Born to be Bound

Alpha's Claim, Book One

By

Addison Cain

ISBN-13: 978-1-950711-13-0

Cover art by Simply Defined Art

Chapter 1

She had made it this far... wide eyes peered through the narrow slit between wool cap and layer upon layer of dingy muffler wrapped around the lower half of her face. No one seemed to be paying much attention as she passed, ignoring the creature in the stinking, oversized coat when it hesitated at the bottom of broad stairs and looked up at Thólos Citadel. Clutching tighter to the bottle of pills in her pocket, madly gripping her lifeline, she took the first step.

For two days, she had taken one of those priceless pills every four hours like clockwork. Walking into what had once been a restricted area, she should have been saturated in the medication, her metabolism and hormones deceived into complacency. A week's worth of food had been traded so she could make the climb up those steps without being torn to pieces.

She was still mortally afraid.

The roar of the monsters inside—the cheers and heckling as her people were stripped of their dignity, then stripped of their lives—turned her stomach, though the acid feeling may have been a side-effect of the drugs. Already sweating, grateful others had covered her in so many layers to hide what she was, Claire took the smallest of breaths, tried not to gag from the stink of rotting corpse that had seasoned her clothes, and walked into madness.

Crossing the entrance was almost too easy. There was no hand gripping her shoulder to cease her movement, no barking Follower demanding she state her business. In fact, the black hole seemed only too willing to suck her in. Over the threshold, the air was ripe with the scent of men; a pungent mixture of aggressive Alpha and some of the more violent Betas who had come to snarl and yip at whoever was that day's entertainment.

Birth titles littered the ground, parchment showing tread marks where uncaring boots had trampled what had once signified a life. A tally of names that had been stricken from the books. The scraps of paper were tossed away to mix with discarded flyers, wanted signs, and garbage.

The deeper she went, the more packed each chamber grew, filled by a horde borne of citizens and the castoff Undercroft scum set free the day terror breached Thólos. They were thugs who had taken up the banner of the Dome's conqueror, men with the power to do as they pleased. Men encouraged to do whatever they pleased. Evil men.

She had to be quick, knowing that if the jostling mob discovered what she was under the stinking filth wrapped around her, she'd die horribly, and all the others would be left to starve. One foot after another, back pressed against the wall, eyes darting to and fro, Claire skirted the crowd and prayed to remain unnoticed.

The male Claire sought had a reputation for standing where any could reach him. Where all could see who held power, so challengers could be killed—if rumors held true—with his bare hands.

One could not have missed him if they tried.

The villain who had the audacity to call himself 'The Shepherd' was massive, the largest Alpha she had ever seen. And not only that... the Da'rin markings. Whatever they were, they swirled over sun-darkened skin as if an extension of his wrongness—animalistic, unnatural. The intricacy of the patterns drew the eye straight to muscled arms, warning all who looked that the bearer was treacherous—not to be trusted.

Before her city had fallen, to bear those shifting black marks above ground had been highly illegal—the punishment: execution. He was a convict of the Undercroft, the one who'd liberated the castoffs, and he was the monster responsible for the suffering of her people and for the corpses piling in the streets of Thólos.

Claire swallowed, creeping nearer, choosing to look instead at the armored Follower Shepherd nodded at; a Da'rin marked Beta, from the look of him. It was that man whose sharp blue eyes caught her creeping nearer. Though diminutive was a gentle way to describe Claire, from his expression, the Beta found her to be nothing... less than nothing. He looked away, dismissing her approach.

Gripping those pills, her talisman against evil, Claire walked straight up to the two conversing conquerors. Seeking the giant Alpha's attention, she fought for the words. "I need to speak with you, please."

Shepherd didn't even look at her, blatantly ignoring the swathed female in her stinking clothes.

"It's very important," she tried a little louder, the sincerity in her eyes, the desperation and overwhelming fear apparent.

How many times had this happened in her life? The total disregard, the blatant rejection...

Claire released a frustrated sigh and clutched her pills even tighter. Standing like a tree, a small sapling in a forest of redwoods, she waited and watched him. There was no way she was leaving until she'd spoken with the only person who might be able to save them. He wanted to be a leader, he wanted to rule... well, they needed food. Pride had only lasted so long. Deep down she knew it would not keep them alive, so she'd come to Shepherd to ask for help.

Eyes trained on the man, on the largest in the room—maybe in the world—she waited for hours. It was hard to ignore what was taking place around her. The weeping of the once mighty reduced to sniveling wretches, dragged in to be held accountable. Claire was unsure what they were being held accountable for. All she knew was that everyone unfortunate enough to be hauled to the Citadel was executed, regardless of begging, bribery, bloodlines... nothing mattered to the mob. Not even guilt.

It grew dark. Claire remained, drawing in those same tiny breaths, holding her ground when all she wanted was to run screaming. Pretend she had not just heard a stranger be sentenced to have his skin

4

peeled off so the world could see what he was made of underneath. It had grown so late, her sad bravery seemed pointless. Not once had those silver eyes turned towards her. Not once.

Claire had hoped her determination would draw Shepherd to at least glance her way as his follower had, giving her a chance to plead her case. Yet the longer she waited, the more her heart began to beat erratically. For a moment, she felt she might vomit from the smell—not just of her clothes, but of all the Alphas raging in the room—and drew out her pills. With the quickest speed she could manage, she opened the lid of the bottle and pinched a little blue tablet between her forefinger and thumb. Her gloved pinky hooked the dirty muffler, pulling it down just enough to get that pill between her lips. Once it hit her tongue, Claire fought to create enough saliva to swallow.

It was jagged passing down her esophagus, made her cringe, then groan when the feeling of it hitting a hollow stomach almost made the precious pharmaceutical come right back up. Her fingers quickly readjusted the wool to cover as much of her skin as possible, pulling the reeking smell back over her nose and mouth... but then everything went wrong.

The very air altered and a shot of instinctual fear was the precursor of her greatest nightmare. It was Shepherd, suddenly unnaturally still. She could hear the bones crack in his neck as he turned his skull a few more degrees in her direction.

Sweating profusely, feeling so ill, Claire spoke the instant she felt his attention. "I must speak to you."

He had killed so many people. Even through the fabric around her face, she could smell him; more potent than the others, for certain. But the look in his eyes was far more frightening than the Da'rin marking. Hard, unforgiving mercury seemed to see right through her, shredding away her disguise. Shoulders drooping, Claire felt a rush, a burning scratch in her stomach that turned into painful cramping, total terror left in its wake.

Everything had been for nothing.

Sucking in a ragged breath, swaying as if her legs could not decide which way to run, Claire whispered under her breath, "No... no, no, this can't be happening."

Somehow, all the preparations, the pills, had not been enough. There were too many Alphas, too much of their scent in the air, and she had gone directly into heat. Already she could feel the slick gathering between her legs, the smell of it, of something so laced with pheromones that it would not be masked by the horrid stench she'd purposely dressed in. All those hours she'd thought it had been lack of food, the stink of rotting things, and the weight of the cloak... she'd stood there in the wolves' den like an idiot while the signs had been building: nausea, racing heart, fever... and the biggest wolf of all was staring straight at her.

Claire finally had his attention, and now it was worthless.

She was already becoming delirious, panicked, her voice cracking and accusing all at once. "I just needed to speak with you. I only needed a minute."

That urge—the one she had fought her whole life—was making her tremble and prepare to flee, but there was already a commotion all around. She tried to hold her breath as Alphas sniffed the air like bloodhounds. Shepherd countered her mincing retreat, facing her full on, staring at her with the wide, focused eyes of a predator.

It was his attention—the attention she had needed to save her kind—that drew other eyes in the room. More of that damn fluid began to drip down her legs, saturating the fabric of her clothing, signaling that a rare Omega had appeared out of the blue, and that she was broadcasting a heat cycle.

There would be a riot, a bloodbath as they pulled at her... probably mounting her right there on that dirty marble floor.

Another cramping wave and she doubled over, her pupils slowly eating up green irises until only black with an emerald ring remained. A roar came from behind, tight grasping hands clutched at her arm. She screamed, and the frenzy began.

Alphas were dominant. They had an animal need to mate an Omega in heat. Self-control, they possessed that, too... but not the monsters who were in the room. Not the kind of men who were attracted to Shepherd's cause. Not what the men in Thólos had become since that bastard descended upon them. She would be raped to death, could already feel someone tearing at her clothes.

Her body's response, Claire could not prevent. The snarls and barks only drew out more slick, made her crave to be mounted... but not by anything that was crawling in that chamber.

A howl so deafening she covered her ears, shook her to the bone. There was the sound of a struggle, gunfire, Claire instinctively curling in on herself.

Fighting her response, forcing her body to straighten so she could do more than yank away from clutching hands, she opened her eyes, exposed blown pupils, and prepared to run. They would chase her, she knew that. Alphas were stronger, fast, and being that she was surrounded, one would catch her. But at least she would have tried.

Claire was unprepared to see the amount of bodies already littering the ground. The sight of so many broken men made her freeze, and that was all he needed. In an instant, an arm as thick as a tree trunk came around her middle, and she was carted off, hanging doubled over, by the swaggering pace of a man staking claim... of the victor of the battle. The room still echoed with snarls and shouting, but more so, the pained moans of the few on the ground who were lucky enough to be alive.

Combat boots and familiar armor, all looking as if they'd been cobbled together from scraps, encased thick thighs. Shepherd. Praising Nona for the horrible stinking scarf she'd prepared, Claire fought herself—fought her instinct to smell him—and did her best to repeat the mantra that had gotten her through this nightmare before. "Only instincts."

She had to speak to him, had to fight her baser urges.

Do you think he will fight his?

The thought made her sag, an action he no doubt took as submission, and not its counterpart, despair. Claire lost track of the distance or direction he had taken her, only noticing the dimness and the strange feeling of being underground. Over and over in her head she prepared what must be said, promising herself she would say it. Even if he was rutting, she would say it.

Even if he would kill her, she would say it.

A door was pulled open on thick metal hinges, whining the way she imagined the doors would in the old-world submarines she'd read about in books, and they entered a room.

Every inhalation, even through the reeking muffler, was saturated in him—in the heady musk of the prime Alpha. Pressing her hand to her mouth and nose, she felt her body writhe against her will, and focused again on the small shallow breaths of control.

Lowered to the floor, her body convulsed in another cramp, drawing out the female's pained groan. She wanted—no, needed—to press her hands between her legs. But the smell of rotting flesh was turning her stomach, just as much as the delicious smell of the Alpha's den was driving her mad.

With words made bleary by craving, sentences broken up by little grunts, she fought past the overwhelming desire to spread her legs and grind. "We are starving. The Omegas need food. I have been sent to ask you to arrange a safe place where we can procure our portion before we all die."

She watched him bolt the door with a rod so thick it dwarfed her ankle, trapping her, cornering the Omega for mating. Unsure if Shepherd had heard, she used her feet to scoot away from the male until her back hit the wall, and tried again. "Food... we can't go out... hunted, forced. They're killing us." Her blown pupils looked up at the intimidating male and pleaded for him to understand. "You are the Alpha in Thólos, you hold control... we have no one else to ask."

"So you foolishly walked into a room full of feral males to ask for food?" He was mocking her, his eyes mean, even as he grinned.

The horror of the day, the sexual frustration of her heat, made Claire belligerently raise her head and meet his eyes. "If we don't get food, I'm dead anyway."

Seeing the female grimace through another cramping wave, Shepherd growled, an instinctual reaction to a breeding Omega. The noise shot right between her legs, full of the promise of everything she needed. His second, louder grumbled noise sang inside her, and a wave of warm slick drenched the floor below her swollen sex, saturating the air to entice him.

She could not take it. "Please don't make that noise."

"You are fighting your cycle," he grunted low and abrasive, beginning to pace, watching her all the while.

Shaking her head back and forth, Claire began to murmur, "I've lived a life of celibacy."

Celibacy? That was unheard of... a rumored story. Omegas could not fight the urge to mate. That was why the Alphas fought for them and forced a pair-bond to keep them for themselves. The smell alone drove any Alpha into a rut.

He growled again and the muscles of her sex clenched so hard she whined and curled up on the floor.

It was hard enough to make it through estrous locked in a room alone until the cycle broke, but his damn noise and the smell invading past the rotting stickiness of her clothing was breaking her insides apart.

The degrading way he spoke made her open her eyes to see the beast standing still, his massive erection apparent despite layers of clothing. "How long does your heat typically last, Omega?"

Shivering, suddenly loving the sound of that lyrical rasp, she clenched her fists at her sides instead of beckoning him nearer. "Four days, sometimes a week."

"And you have been through them all in seclusion instead of submitting to an Alpha to break them?"

"Yes."

11

He was making her angry, furious even, with his stupid questions. Every part of her was screaming out that he should be stroking her and easing the need. That it was his job! With her hand still pressed over her nose and mouth, her muffled, broken explanation came as a jumbled, angry rant, Claire hissing, "I choose."

He just laughed, a cruel, coarse sound.

Omegas had become exceptionally rare since the plagues and the following Reformation Wars a century prior. That made them a valuable commodity which Alphas in power took as if it was their due. And in a city brimming with aggressive Alphas like Thólos, she'd been trapped in a life of feigning existence as a Beta just to live unmolested, spent a small fortune on heat-suppressants, and locked herself away with the other few celibates she knew when estrous came. Hidden in plain sight before Shepherd's army sprung out of the Undercroft and the government was slaughtered, their corpses left strung up from the Citadel like trophies.

Claire had been forced into hiding the very next day, when the unrest inspired the lower echelons of population to challenge for dominance. Where there had been order, suddenly all Thólos knew was anarchy. Those awful men just took any Omega they could find, killing mates and children in order to keep the women—to breed them or fuck until they died.

"What is your name?"

She opened her eyes, elated he was listening. "Claire."

"How many of you are there, little one?"

12

Trying to focus on a spot on the wall instead of the large male and where his beautiful engorged dick was challenging the zipper of his trousers, she turned her head to where her body craved to nest, staring with hunger at the collection of colorful blankets, pillows—a bed where everything must be saturated by his scent.

An extended growl warned, "You are losing your impressive focus, little one. How many?"

Her voice broke. "Less than a hundred... We lose more every day."

"You have not eaten. You're hungry." It was not a question, but spoken with such a low vibration that his hunger for her was apparent.

"Yesss." It was almost a whine. She was so near to pleading, and it wasn't going to be for food.

The prolonged answering growl of the beast compelled a gush of slick to wet her so badly, she was left sitting in a slippery puddle. Doubling over, frustrated and needy, she sobbed, "Please don't make that noise," and immediately the growl changed pitch. Shepherd began to purr for her.

There was something so infinitely soothing in that low rumble that she sighed audibly and did not bolt at his slow, measured approach. She watched him with such attention, her huge, dilated pupils a clear mark that she was so very close to falling completely into estrous.

Even when Shepherd crouched down low, he towered over her, all bulging muscle and musky sweat. She tried to say the words, "Only instincts..." but jumbled them so badly their meaning was lost.

Starting with the scarf, he unwound the items that tainted her beautiful pheromones, purring and stroking every time she whimpered or shifted nervously. When he pulled her forward to take away the reeking cloak, her eyes drew level with his confined erection. Claire's uncovered nose sniffed automatically at the place where his trousers bulged. In that moment all she wanted, all that she had ever wanted, was to be fucked, knotted, and bred by that male.

Only instincts...

Shepherd pressed his face to her neck and sucked in a long breath, groaning as his cock jumped and began to leak to please her. He had gone into the rut, there was no changing that fact, and with it came a powerful need to see the female filled with seed, to soothe what was driving her to rub against her hand in such a frenzy.

The words were almost lost in her breath, "You need to lock me in a room for a few days..."

A feral grin spread. "You are locked in a room, little one, with the Alpha who killed ten men and two of his sworn Followers to bring you here." He stroked her hair, petting her because something inside told him his hands could calm her. "It's too late now. Your defiant celibacy is over. Either you submit willingly to me where I will rut you through your heat, or you may leave out that door where my men will, no doubt, mount you in the halls once they smell you."

14

A knock came. Shepherd rose up tall before her, staring down with open demand that she submit and obey. Dominance established, he went to the door and pulled back the lock. Claire saw the same soldier, the smaller Beta with the far too vibrant blue eyes, and found him sniffing the air in her direction, growing openly excited at the intoxicating blend of pheromones her slick and sweat were pumping into the air.

Shepherd was right. He had taken her from what would have been a mass rape, saved her from damage and most likely death. He'd listened, though he had not answered her, and men were already salivating in the hall. The understanding of the situation passed openly across her face. Claire nodded, estrous clouding her judgment.

Something was muttered between the men, ending in, "...only Betas on guard."

A tray was handed over, laden with food, another armful piled with bedding and pillows, and she went white. They had already known Shepherd would have her, and had prepared accordingly. The little chat had no purpose but to make her think she had a choice. He saw her expression and the rumble of his purring returned.

She had to eat... he had to feed her before it began. The tray was set on the floor where she crouched, his order loud enough to grab her attention away from where his pants bulged. "Eat."

As she picked at the unseen food, he began to undress. All armor, every under-layer, was carefully removed and organized, the man having no shame about the state of his Da'rin marked body or the jutting cock proudly on display. But more than the visual, it was the smell—the scent of a rutting Alpha, aroused and swollen for her—that made reason completely flee her mind. Everything hummed in that incessant purr, reminding her that he was what her body needed, and she was salivating for it... even if she was scared.

Shepherd began to pace, naked, rolling his shoulders as he prowled, all the while watching her and sniffing the air over and over. "Eat more... drink the water."

Voice downright nasty, threatening, Claire hissed as if he should have known Omegas could not eat during estrous, "I don't want food!"

No, she wanted the thing that was supposed to happen. He was supposed to be fucking her. Why was he waiting? She came to her feet and he was there, the dominant male growling so loud her eyes rolled back in her skull.

A rending of fabric preceded cool air over fevered skin.

He was all around her, tugging away unnecessary things like clothing. The smell of him, the raw sweat, sent her cunt to seeping. Sucking in great panting breaths of the fertile Omega, Shepherd sought out to stroke uncovered flesh, a bit surprised all her body hair had been permanently removed— recognizing the precaution the Omega had taken to help mask her scent.

She was so far gone, her little tongue already licking at his skin, completely high on the taste and

16

smell, that when his finger swiped drops of his leaking pre-come to run over her lips, she moaned loudly and sucked it deep into her mouth.

Claire was so small compared to his mass, easy to move where he wanted. Her back hit the bed, Shepherd standing between her slender spread legs, staring down with wide, hungry eyes at the river of slick that came forth. Little pink lips were spread, the swollen glans of his cock lined up where she seemed far too small to accept an organ so large. With one hand on her chest, petting the twisting thing, Shepherd pressed forward, breaching her slippery womb, and gave a full body shudder at the sound of her desperate cry.

The woman had not lied... she was so tight it made his cock pulsate more fluid to aid her. He only got halfway before she began to whine and squirm. Alphas were big and Shepherd was huge, his girth massive, and there was only so much space inside her body.

"Open for me, little one," Shepherd growled, using his thumbs to stretch her lower lips further apart, thrusting forward, gaining hard earned inch by inch while the female watched a cock as thick as her forearm slowly disappear between her legs.

When the expanding thrust bottomed out, when all her tightness enveloped that hard length... utter bliss. She needed it, was moaning and arching, grinding her sex against his pubic bone. The stretch was divine, the vibration from his purrs, the smell. When he began to pull out, she showed her teeth and snarled at a man many times her size. Shepherd

17

seemed amused, and then snapped his hips, burying that massive cock to the hilt, knowing she would squeal.

Claire learned quickly that he liked her little spurts of temper, but it was Shepherd who dominated the exchange. He rutted with the vigor she needed, hard and fast, building up that furious pulse in her core. When she began to roll her hips, eyes closed and lost in the insatiable need to mate, he took her by the scruff of the neck and barked at her to open, to look at the male fucking her, to recognize his prowess.

Those harshly snarled words sent her over the edge. Perfect fulfillment exploded. Claire felt every single muscle in her pussy jump to life, saw his eyes grow vicious and feral, felt his knot expand as he ground in, hooking behind her pelvic bone, locking them as deep as he could go. Jerking under the intensity of the orgasm, she felt that first hot gush of semen, heard him roar like a beast while she screamed. Shepherd came again, more of that copious fluid, her body's need finally met, and with his third liquid surge, she blacked out.

It could not have been long before she woke, as his knot was still binding their bodies together. He lay below her, her body sprawled on top, Claire's ear to his heart. The serenity from the mating was fading and the impulse to fuck was back again. The urge, the only thing that defined her at that moment, grew beyond her when her tongue darted out to lick the salt of sweat from his chest, to entice the tattooed male to begin again.

The instant the knot began to diminish, she registered the loss of precious fluid, felt his seed leaking out of her, and whined. As if knowing her thoughts, Shepherd dragged his fingers in the little river and brought his ejaculate to her mouth. The smell alone drove her wild, the taste a thousand times more.

"They would have broken an Omega so small." Shepherd watched, fascinated, as she greedily sucked his fingers, explaining quietly as if educating a female who should have known better. "Not shown restraint at a scent so overpowering."

She didn't want him to talk. She wanted him to fuck her again. A large hand came to her hair, rubbing at the scalp of the female, soothing her with pets and purrs while the knot slowly abated so he could thrust against her jerking hips.

The second mating was much less frantic, far more fulfilling, and when he had filled her again, Claire began to lose the edge that was making her so ferocious. It was his hands, maybe, lifting and lowering her at the tempo that made her cunt sing, or the look in his eyes, the unabashed lustful pleasure.

So that's what it was like to mate an Alpha.

He seemed to know her thoughts, and by the crinkles at the corner of Shepherd's eyes, she could tell he was amused with her. He cupped her face, tender and gentle, and she didn't feel overpowered or forced... She felt mistakenly safe in the delirium.

It was not until a day later, when he took her from behind at the peak of estrous, his full weight on her back, that she sensed trouble. The high had not faded, the slow building fervor of her heat nowhere near breaking... but he roared, began to squeeze and bruise; to restrain her. Fighting the hold, writhing, Claire had a sobering fear the tyrant might bite her so savagely it would scar—that he intended to leave claiming marks.

Worst of all, instinctively, she wanted him to. Her estrous-high mind wanted to bond to the monster that had destroyed Thólos and made her life hell, simply because he was the one who was fucking her.

"And you will!" he growled in her ear.

She told him no, panting it over the sound of his skin slapping against the fleshy mounds of her ass. Sharp teeth came to her shoulder, Shepherd's knot growing bulbous until the Alpha could no longer thrust and she could not squirm away. She screamed in pain and pleasure, sobbing as his teeth ripped into her skin, Shepherd growling long and low with her flesh torn from his bite.

She climaxed from the claiming, rhythmically squeezing, drawing the jets of fluid from his dick while he crooned at her and lapped up the blood.

Claire cried even as he purred and petted, wept from the hazy recognition of the total loss of control she'd so carefully cultivated in her life. When ten minutes later her body sent out signals it was time for Shepherd to fuck her again, he pulled her beneath him and was gentle, caressing the woman he'd stolen even though her tears fell throughout the whole coupling.

When it was over, when he had wrung out another explosion that chased away the urge of chemical madness, a calm descended on them both. Claire briefly slept against a man she did not know, pressing as close as she could, in the exact place the brute expected her to rest.

***

In the end, it took three days to break the starving Omega's heat. She was sleeping, nesting deep into the blankets covered in his semen and her slick—blissed out. Toying with a strand of her sooty black hair, Shepherd mulled over just what to do with what was now his possession, impressed that the little female was plucky enough to dress in a corpse's clothing and parade into a pack of Alphas just to speak to him. She would have died if he had not found her scent worth killing for.

Claire would also be sore now that estrous had ended, and her mind was not clouded with the insatiable drive to mate. He was certain she would also be resentful of the binding he'd forced. But that was the lot for Omegas, the way of nature. He wanted her, he took. End of story.

Silver eyes ran over the lithe dancer's body she possessed, the Alpha growling at the obvious fact his Omega was underfed. It was getting him into such a mood that, when a knock came to the door, he covetously grabbed what was his and roared.

The commotion—being jerked against a mountain of heat—woke Claire, and she hissed in discomfort. Everything felt sticky, a male pawing over bruises that did not appreciate the attention. The words he spat were in another language—an outskirts' lost tongue, she assumed. Remembering who he was and what he'd done to her, she pushed away from Shepherd's chest, only to feel his arms grow impossibly constrictive. The conversation between the Follower on the other side of the door and her captor stretched on, Shepherd tightening his grip each time she squirmed.

When it was over, Shepherd swung his skull her way, barking, "You need to sleep more." It was not a suggestion, and she could clearly sense he was provoked.

"The Omegas." That was the reason she had come to him... not to have him knot her for three full days.

Mercurial eyes diminished between narrowed lids. Shepherd sniffed her once, then he growled, "Your assumption it would be plausible to have a private distribution of provisions is flawed. It would only draw attention to your group. All Omegas will be delivered into my care and segregated from the population in the Undercroft. Should any come into heat, an Alpha will be chosen from amongst my Followers. Most will be bonded at their next estrous."

"What? No!" Claire's voice was pure horror. "That's not what we want. They need food, not to be made into slaves."

"This is best. You are Omegas, fragile, and it is not your place to decide such things."

Everything about the male was suddenly repulsive. Claire wanted him off of her and tried to scoot away. "I won't tell you where they are."

As he smirked, a scar across his lips made the expression sinister. "Then they will starve and be picked off one by one. That is your decision, little one. If given to me, they would be protected."

"From whom? The very men who are raping and knotting girls who have not reached maturity are the same you surround yourself with."

Shepherd was petting her, touching her hair as if she were not upset, as if she didn't loathe him in that moment, and it was setting her into a temper. When she tried to bat his hand away, he snarled and pinned her beneath him. His teeth went to the crook of her neck and he smelled, growling at the sweetness while using his thigh to pry her legs apart.

Claire felt his cock pulsing against her belly and grew frightened. There was no estrous, no abundant slick, and she was sore. Shepherd didn't care. He reminded her who was dominant in one sharp thrust, taking his Omega with no purrs or caresses, knotting without her climax to urge his seed forth. When the powerful spurts bathed her womb, there was no settling peace, only frustration and tears.

When he seemed to have caught his breath, the unwelcome press of his mouth came to her ear. "You will sleep more."

His fingers went back to toying with her hair while Claire cried herself beyond exhaustion, embraced by a man who lived up to his reputation as a monster.

23

Chapter 2

It was dark the next time she woke. Though Shepherd was not physically there, he was still humming inside her. The new bond stuck like a greasy string to her ribcage, burrowing steadily. Claire had only heard descriptions of the pair-bond and read about it in the Archives. Each Omega experienced the link differently. Some compared it to a wellspring—an endless offering of cool water—others to a knife wound that tore and twisted their insides. Hers felt like a worm, writhing and going deeper. A subjugation and a leash. She already hated it. It was unwelcome, invasive, and something she could not ignore.

At that moment, it hummed in an off-putting, out of tune twang. Like a bad note on a violin.

Feeling her way around the walls in search of a switch, Claire stumbled into unfamiliar furniture and cursed. The feeling of the bathroom door came under her fingers. She went inside and flicked on the light.

Her reflection stared back at her.

Naked and so covered in Shepherd's semen it was caked in her hair, she looked shattered. In the hazy, blissful high of their frenzy, he'd fed it to her, rubbed it into her skin—saturated her inside and out with that viscous liquid. If he had not spent so much time running his fingers through her hair, she was certain it would have been a matted mess.

Disgusted, Claire approached the stranger in the mirror. In the months since she'd last seen her body reflected back at her, she had become so thin. Her ribs protruded, the bones of her hips stuck out. She'd grown skeletal. But it was not the emaciation that won her attention. It was the inflamed bite mark on her shoulder, the swollen red scabs throbbing.

Shepherd had bitten her so deeply she would carry the scar of his claiming forever.

Tracing a finger over the two crescent wounds, Claire felt shame in her ignorance. She didn't fully understand how the bond was formed. A lifetime of concealing her nature had made it dangerous to ask too many questions. All she'd known was that it involved marking and an Alpha's initiation of the act.

Maybe it was just instincts.

Only instincts...

A sinking despair grew in her belly, made worse by the still thrumming string her body was trying to reject. Claire pulled in a deep breath and scanned the rest of the simple lavatory. Either the man was fastidiously tidy or he had an underling clean for him. The sink was gleaming white, the mirror polished, not even a speck of toothpaste on it.

Opening the medicine cabinet, it was almost bizarre to find ordinary things such as a toothbrush and mouthwash. It was the Da'rin markings maybe, the fact he had lived long enough in the Undercroft to garner so many. She'd been taught they were all unwashed savages, less than human.

Wavering between using his toothbrush to get the fuzzy feeling out of her mouth and disgusted because it was his toothbrush, she finally just reached for the damn thing. A few minutes later, her mouth no longer tasted like... things she didn't want to think about. Setting it on the shelf in the exact position she'd found it in, Claire turned towards the shower and cranked it on.

Stepping under a scalding spray, she invited the burn, wanting everything Shepherd off of her. Eyes closed, hair under the stream, she let water pour like lava over her body. The puncture wounds at her shoulder started to ooze, the scabs softening from the moisture.

There was only a basic bar of soap.

Every possible inch was scrubbed until her skin grew raw, every trace of that man and his smell stripped away. She soaped up her hair, dreaming of the days she'd had access to such simple things as shampoo. When it was done, she stepped out of the steam, looking at the man's towel, and chose not to use anything of his that might re-apply his scent to her body.

Skin bumped from the cold, she air-dried, wrung out her hair over the sink, trying her best to finger comb the black mess into order. Paranoid about punishment, she wiped down all traces of her time in that room, leaving it as close to how she'd found it as she could.

With the light from the bathroom streaming into the cell of Shepherd's den, Claire found a table lamp and switched it on. In estrous, her mind had not

27

focused on such paltry things as furniture placement and decoration. All she'd seen was where she wanted to nest and the male waiting to mount her.

After all the years of careful seclusion, all the tortured heat cycles spent locked away to prevent such a thing, it felt like she'd lost a part of herself knowing she had been mated... and not by an Alpha she'd chosen.

Now, she was somehow less. A failure.

That humming little cord in her chest pulsed as if to suggest that she was more... that there was more now. It whispered that Shepherd had only done what was supposed to be done.

The plaguing vibration made her angry. Desperate, she grasped for any potential relief. The pair-bond was still new, it was fragile. Maybe she could break it?

How often had every other forcefully bonded Omega wished for the same thing?

It was almost laughable how quickly the little cord in her chest hummed, tempting her to accept her position, to submit to such a strong Alpha.

The feeling made her want to vomit.

It was unsettling. The change in Shepherd from the coercive beginning to the unquestioned authoritarian frightened her. He had forced a pair-bond, made a choice that would impact the rest of her life. Alphas and Omegas only bonded once, except for extreme cases when mates died. It was Betas who lived without the bond. It was Betas Claire had always envied. They had no estrous and could still bear children. Betas got to choose. They mated at will, some even with the same partner for a lifetime, not from some device of nature that forced a permanent pairing. To make the sting that much greater, unlike Omegas, Beta females were treated with the same respect as Beta males.

Betas were also second in the hierarchy of the three human dynamics. They had freedom to do as they pleased with their lives. Omegas, so rare and highly desired, had been relegated to a prestige of prized pet—a status symbol for powerful Alphas to claim. They were smaller, no less intelligent, but as their numbers were decreasing, it was an easy minority for the rest of the colonies to force into some archaic ideal. The Alphas ruled the last bastions of civilization, were supreme in every Bio-Dome, every regulated quadrant, every powerful business, and there were a lot more of them than there were Omegas.

Looking over the dim room, ignoring the nest she'd built between sessions of being fucked, Claire wondered about the man. Spartan was not exactly the right word for what she saw... maybe utilitarian was better. Only the basics existed: a bed, desk, small table, and a few other useful pieces of furniture; all mismatching, none chosen for anything other than practicality.

Then there was the bookcase.

Stepping barefoot over a concrete floor, she looked at the titles, several of which were in different languages, and found his collection of literature... surprising. These were the books of an intellectual, many clearly having been read more than once. She recognized several of the authors, Nietzsche and Machiavelli to name a few, only because books penned by those men had been banned from the Archives. The penalty for possessing such literature was so severe, even knowing her government had fallen, Claire was nervous to touch them.

Then again, who but Shepherd was going to punish her now?

Limbs shaky from the toll taken on her body during estrous, Claire reached out and traced her finger over the spines. It was cold in that subterranean, windowless space—a reminder that he had dragged her down into the Undercroft. She abandoned her exploration and sought out her clothes... only to find that every last shredded piece was gone.

She would rather face Shepherd's wrath for wearing his clothing without permission than wait around naked like an odalisque. Digging through the room's modest dresser, Claire found a sweater that would pass for a dress on her much smaller frame. Pulling the grey thing over her head, she was relieved to find it clean, the garment holding only the faintest trace of his scent.

Stomach rumbling, she began to pace, her eyes inadvertently looking toward the part of the room saturated in the dried reek of their combined estrous emissions: her nest. Claire had built them before in seclusion—it was an obsessive part of the heat-cycle, everything arranged just so. Blankets, pillows, all forming the shape that best suited the

Omega. That made the females, or in the extraordinary exception the Omega was male, feel safe. The idea of nests had always fascinated her, the way she knew exactly where every piece should fit, the comfort she took in lying in the finished product; even though the ones she'd created in seclusion had never been used to mate.

Betas didn't nest. And base Alphas, or so she'd heard, would mount any Omega without allowing the nest, in a frenzy to begin the seeding. Proper Alphas understood the necessity. Shepherd had let her build it, had supplied extra blankets and materials aside from the usual things already on his bed. He'd even tried to help, crouched naked at her side, tugging fabric and fluffing pillows to hand to her. When he'd become too involved, she'd snarled and pushed his hands away. The nest was her job. He was an Alpha; his only job was to fuck her in it.

Her first mated nest was supposed to be something beyond special, a cherished memory, and not a thing that made her eyes well each time she foolishly glanced in its direction.

There was nothing special about the fluid crusted, sticky arrangement she had woken up in.

Frowning, Claire looked away before she screamed. The door was in her line of sight, one metal blockade between her and air that did not stink of sex. Pacing again, she tried to steady the wave of horror in her gut. The lack of windows, not knowing if it was day or night, feeling trapped underground, was itching uncomfortably under her skin. She didn't even know where she was in relation to the Dome.

31

The longer she walked the length of the room, the more she wanted out of it.

She ran to the door and tried the knob, knowing it would be locked but needing to feel the immovable metal with her own fingers. The cry she made was unavoidable. A sad whimper of someone who'd hoped. Someone on the verge of panic. She was a prisoner bound to a man she did not know, hungry, scared, and suffering an unwelcome thread that would not stop existing no matter how hard she willed it away.

By the time her captor returned, Claire was stretched out on the floor, staring at the ceiling with glassy eyes.

"You have been distressed," Shepherd grunted, sniffing the air. "Because you are hungry?"

Blinking at the ceiling, wondering if he could feel just what she was thinking at that moment, Claire glanced past his massive legs to the door that was now unlocked, and imagined she might make a run for it, that freedom was hers.

"I see," he growled, eyes narrowed to slits.

As the breath left her lungs, she admitted, "I am very hungry."

Crouching over her, he found her green eyes had shifted under her scowl. "You woke sooner than I anticipated."

There were a million things she wanted to shout. Instead, all she did was give a forlorn sigh. "I don't know what time of day it is."

"It is the midday hour. Food will arrive shortly."

"Grand." Claire's attention went back to the cement ceiling.

The male went so far as to run his fingers over her pouting lips. "Do you have any desire to mate?"

"I do not," she answered quickly, still frightened from the last painful coupling. It was all Claire could do to fight the urge to scoot away, certain it would only entice him to chase and do it again.

Small crinkles formed at the corner of Shepherd's eyes, the bastard smug. The softest of purrs began, and in answer, her scowl somewhat lessened. The unconscious reaction annoyed her, even more so when his hand burrowed into her hair, pulling gently at the roots, and her eyes mechanically closed with the wave of contentment that came with each little tug.

By the time a sharp knock came to the door, she was a puddle on the floor.

Shepherd called for the familiar Beta to enter, continuing to pet his female while his Follower set out a tray. Claire wondered if he did it just to make a point to another nearby male, to be possessive, or simply because it seemed to appease her. Probably all three.

They were alone again. The giant gave her a nudge to open her eyes, cocking his head toward the table. "Eat."

He insisted on helping her stand, making her touch him more than she wanted. Glancing at the delicious smelling tray, Claire found that there was only food for her. Throughout the meal, he watched her as one watches prey, noting the minutiae of her movements. She didn't like canned green beans, but she ate what was given. She hummed at the taste of ham. The glass of milk made her lips curl just a little.

There was a pill on the side of the tray, a thing she had seen, then forgotten—too caught up in an actual warm meal. Shepherd's large fingers pinched it and held it out for her to take.

"What is that?" Claire asked, covering her mouth as she spoke.

"You are deficient in many nutrients from starvation and recent estrous."

There was no point in arguing. Whether it was a vitamin or poison, if he wanted her to take it, it would be a simple thing for him to force.

As she swallowed the tablet, Shepherd said, "The blue pills I found in your coat pocket. Do you know what they were?"

Disgust was clear in her expression. "They were supposed to be heat-suppressants—cost me a week's worth of food. I had been taking them for days before I came to the Citadel to beg for your help. Clearly, they didn't work, and you didn't help, either. So... as far as I see it, they were a bad joke."

Reaching across the table for her free hand, Shepherd wrapped his great paw around her wrist. All he need do was squeeze and her bones would be crushed and broken. She took it as a subtle warning to watch her tongue.

Tracing his thumb over her pulse, he explained, "I had a lab analyze your pills. They were quite the opposite, little one—designed to prompt your heat-cycle."

Opposite? Fertility drugs... Other girls in hiding had been taking those pills. Dozens of the Omegas could have gone into heat unexpectedly, exposed, just as she had been. That was exactly the point he was trying to make.

With her head in her hand, she heard him outline precisely what she was already thinking. "Someone clever is using your needs to hunt down the Omegas. They know the females taking those pills believe in their effectiveness and don't anticipate they'll go into heat out in the open. And like you, they will be mobbed, hunted down, or taken."

"That's barbaric. You men are so fucking evil..."

Shepherd knew it was a generalized collective of males she was referring to, not him specifically, and did not allow more than a hint of anger to come through his voice. "Where did you get them?"

After a deep breath, she admitted, "From the same men peddling drugs on the causeways. Anyone has access to them. I approached as a Beta, covered in the smell of another."

"The smell of another?"

"Those who are strong enough to leave our hiding place steal the clothes from the dead rotting on

35

the streets. We use their scent to hide our own, as you must have noticed when I came to you. It is unpleasant, but we need supplies, we need food. We do what we have to, to survive."

"Why was a young female chosen to approach the Citadel and not someone older, with less chance of entering estrous or attracting attention?" Shepherd demanded.

"I volunteered."

"Why?"

"I am healthier than most of the others, have lived for years passing myself off as a Beta, and am trusted to think objectively for the collective as I have no mate or children."

"You have a mate," he reminded her, releasing her wrist to brush the sore bite mark he'd left on her shoulder. "I claimed you. You belong to me now."

Her stomach churned and she worried her lip. Looking up into his steady silver eyes, she whispered, "You could change your mind."

For a split second, Shepherd seemed a little disappointed. An instant later, he grew viciously determined. "I am not an impulsive man. I made a decision. What was done is done. I claimed you. You are mine now. That is all."

"But you don't even know me," Claire tried to explain, realizing the male couldn't care less about something as inconsequential as the personality of a female who would be compelled by the bond to be his mate. Her wishes no longer mattered.

In a low, enticing purr he explained, "It's amazing the things you learn about the female writhing on your cock for three days."

Blushing up to her roots, Claire hid her face back in her hand.

Shepherd hooked a finger under her chin and brought her flushed expression up to examine. Tracing the pink on her cheeks, he said, "For example, you were pure... had not wasted yourself on the first Alpha to cross you in a heat. You also have a strong will for a member of a submissive collective."

"It's not submission if you're forced!"

"If you had behaved, I would not have punished you."

The way he spoke, the low rasped words, brought back all her fear. "I didn't want you to touch me—"

With eyes still dangerously narrowed, Shepherd leaned across the table until they were nose to nose. "I will touch you when I wish, any way I wish."

All the accumulating stress, the horror, the rage, just made her snap. "I do not want to be tied to a brute, to be pawed at and raped by a stranger—especially a male who wants me to sell my kind into sexual slavery!" Claire could hardly believe she had screamed out her feelings, and instantly pressed her hand over her mouth, staring at the seething male with frightened eyes.

There was no question of what was coming next. Shepherd stood and plucked her from her seat, returning to the nest they had created in her heat. He ripped the stolen shirt from over her head and already began to peel out of his clothing.

It was unfair how easily he could subdue her. Claire was pressed naked into the cold, sticky fabric, trembling, but too proud to apologize or beg. It would have been pointless anyway. Shepherd's naked weight came upon her, his hand cupping one swollen breast, tweaking her nipple until she squirmed.

Shepherd growled, his voice monstrous, "Raped? You screamed and begged, little one. You scratched and snarled if I did not fuck you when you wanted to be mounted. Have you forgotten? Shall I remind you?"

His hand dipped between the trembling legs his thick thighs spread open. She was dry as a desert until he pressed his chest to hers, put his scarred lips at her ear, and let out the slow animal growl that caused her to gush. Her folds grew slick, her body instinctively answering the call of her Alpha. He tugged and teased her labia, spreading her secretions, circling the nub of nerves at the apex of her sex while the Omega wriggled pointlessly in an attempt to get away. She was twitching each time he pinched her little bud, so frustrated and outraged that, when his cock was jammed inside her, she screamed. Her cry was far more than aggravated anger. It was positively dripping with the unwanted hunger the growls and touches her paired Alpha forced on her.

Holding her hands pinned by her head, Shepherd began to pump his hips, his silver eyes locked on hers. He made that growl again, felt her juices around his cock, and grinned. Each thrust filled that slippery vise, stretching, and making the thread hum with a sense of completion. When it was too much, when Claire couldn't hold back the waves of compelled ecstasy, she called out her hatred, cursing him to the pits of hell, between pleasured gasps and long moans. Shepherd just laughed and fucked her harder, pistoning his hips the way he'd learned his little Omega liked best.

With a wanton moan, she came, still calling out obscenities, full of coerced rapture until only his name was on her lips.

"Shepherd..."

The knot grew, his cock forced as deep as it could go the instant her muscles began clenching rhythmically to draw out his seed. Watching him grunt like a beast, Claire felt the thick spurted ropes of cream, lost in the rapture of her greedy pussy milking his cock until she was pooling with the stuff.

While the knot persisted, Shepherd looked into disoriented green eyes and demanded roughly, "Whose name did you call as you came?"

Claire could hardly breathe, was on the ebb of a powerful climax that shook her to her bones. She whispered, trying not to cry, "Yours."

"Because I am your Alpha." It was almost a roar. "You want to be fucked by me! Do you understand?"

Shaking her head, her lower lip quivering, Claire spoke the truth. "I don't understand."

39

Unfazed by the challenge, Shepherd coldly said, "Then allow me to show you again."

Once the knot subsided, he took her gently, coaxing and stroking, his thrusts slow and calculating. He played her body like a violin, drew out every possible sound a pleased female could make, gave her the type of orgasm that builds slow and burns long, watching her as a cat watches a mouse hole.

It continued for hours as he stripped away all her petty convictions until she was too exhausted to fight back, until her hands began to reach for him in a sex-induced daze, to stroke his back and trace the lines of his horrid tattoos. When his point had been thoroughly made, Shepherd held her against him and purred as he petted, rewarding the wayward Omega for coming to heel.

Chapter 3

Shepherd could call it whatever he wanted—animal impulse, compulsion of biology, necessity of the bond—to Claire, it was still rape. She hated herself every time he coerced her to softly murmur his name in the dark, or reached out a hand to stroke the bulge of his muscle.

It was the same every day. He was almost constantly buried inside her womb. He took her when she woke, after she ate, roughly if she seemed irritable. And he always made her climax... simply to prove that he could. It left her boneless and complaisant, shut off the mind screaming at her to remember herself.

And the damn purr; Shepherd exercised it expertly when she paced in frustration or fussed.

Time became irrelevant. Claire was not even sure how long she had been underground, if it had been days or weeks. Anytime she wanted to know the hour she had to ask, and it eventually grew confusing. Night was day, day was night—everything was turned around.

Even the arrival of meals followed no set pattern, though she was never hungry for long. Shepherd was feeding her so much, in fact, it seemed sacrilegious when she could not always empty her plate. The man was fattening her up.

Random things arrived in the room for her use: products for her hair, a brush, clothing of a sort—all dresses worn only by the elite women housed at the warm levels nearest the top of the Dome—but no shoes or underwear. When Shepherd was gone, she slept. Almost the instant she woke, he returned. It was odd—like he knew—like he felt her cycles on his side of the thread. And always, before words were spoken, he took off his clothing, came to the bed, and lay with her.

Claire knew nothing about the man, but had memorized every inch of his body, the random placement of scars, the smoothness of his skin. And she knew how every inch of him tasted. None of the attention was out of affection—it was just part of the spell he would build. Though her tongue might lick his flesh, Claire never once returned any kiss he tried to press against her mouth.

That was one thing he couldn't take and couldn't force.

His expressions were another study, Shepherd conveying much with his steel eyes. Claire was learning to read his moods by their subtle shifts. When he arrived angry, eyes blazing and nostrils flared over something she had no knowledge of, he almost always mounted her from behind—hard and fast—roaring when he came. When he seemed his version of mellow, it was slow touches while he watched her face. What she saw then, the calculation, the intense concentration—it frightened her more. He was dissecting her piece by piece. A little pressure here, a little tug there... and poof, no more Claire.

Their schedules were markedly different. They never shared meals. In fact, she never saw him eat. The only thing he seemed keen to share with her was his bathing ritual, washing her being an act Shepherd enjoyed and took extensive care with. Once she was clean, he would rut immediately. Sometimes against the wall in the shower, as if he could not wait another second to put his scent back on his Omega.

It felt like her vocabulary had been reduced to only soft gasps or screams of, "Shepherd..." That was what he coaxed out. "Shepherd..." Another part of her died... "Shepherd..."

Lying spread on top of him, not knowing the hour or day of the week, Claire felt the anchor of his knot locked inside her and suddenly began to weep as if her heart was breaking.

With his hand stroking her hair, he hummed, half-asleep, "Why are you crying, little one?"

She was crying because he was killing her.

He hushed her and wiped the tears that continued to fall. "What would please you?"

"I want to go outside," she sobbed against his chest, so very tired of those four concrete walls. "I need to see the sky."

There was no answer for a moment, only the sound of his breathing. "Once you have become more settled in your new life, it may be allowed on occasion, but only under escort and only if you have a bellyful of my seed to scent you."

So she would be expected to mate with him just to leave the room. The exploitation was not missed. Her tears dried and her usual distracted dejection made the little string buzz out of tune. "I have done nothing wrong, and you have trapped me in prison."

Shepherd felt her resentment through the thinly formed cord, traced the line of her spine as he considered her opinion of prison and how it was far from the actual truth. His little Omega should be grateful. Life could be a whole lot worse for her. "It isn't safe for you outside this room."

Half aware of what she was saying, Claire lay lifeless and muttered, "Thólos is unsafe because you made it that way."

Silver eyes focused on the strands of midnight hair running through his fingers. "That is true."

With her cheek pressed to his heart, she said, "You're insane."

She felt a bit of a rumbling chuckle and just ignored him.

Shepherd palmed her rear. "You have not been this conversational in some time."

The knot was slowly beginning to loosen, his seed spilling out as the barrier receded. Feeling the gratuitous amount of fluid drip from her womb, she drummed her fingers on his barrel chest. "If I start talking, you throw me on the bed. What's the point?"

"I only quiet you when you fret."

"Like I said... crazy."

"Resisting is pointless," the male grunted, stroking her back to quietness when she seemed eager to wiggle away.

Resigned, Claire stilled and was rewarded with a purr, certain the man was trying to train her like some dog.

"You will find, in time, that the arrangement will naturally grow on you, little one." Shepherd spoke as if he knew, as if it were absolute. "Exercise patience."

Defiant, she growled against his naked chest, "My name is Claire."

He smacked her backside hard enough to sting.

Her head flew up, green eyes blazing. He chuckled, the sound masculine, and musical, and thoroughly entertained. She hated it.

"Don't spank me like a child!"

Silver eyes playful, he refuted, "If you act like one, I will answer accordingly."

"My name is Claire. Claire O'Donnell. And before you unleashed hell in Thólos, I was an artist. I had a life and friends... my own home... things you must imagine an Omega worked very hard to achieve in a world where we are prized for mates but lowest in the hierarchy. You took all that away, stripped every one of us of what we were, made the masses so feral that I had to go into hiding. You might have me trapped, but I will always be Claire."

Seemingly unconcerned with her rant, Shepherd cupped the curve of her hip. "What sort of art?"

Scowling, she answered bluntly, "Illustrations for children's books."

"Given your previous celibacy it seems a bit ironic, don't you think, Miss O'Donnell?"

"Why, because I didn't breed with the first Alpha who sniffed me? I wanted to find a good mate, and the men I've met tend to be..." her eyes held his as she spoke her feelings, "pretty terrible."

Shepherd's expression was not threatening, his silver eyes remained languid, but in a growl, he harshly explained, "You chose to enter the Citadel. You exposed yourself at great risk. You must have known you would never be allowed to return once I knew what you were."

"I was hoping a man known as The Shepherd would have honor," Claire grudgingly admitted.

Voice almost lazy, Shepherd replied, "And I did the honorable thing, did I not? I fought a mob and saved you from violent rape. I gave you a choice. You chose me and I claimed you. Since then, you have been protected and cared for while others suffer under the Dome."

"A choice?" She practically choked on the word. "You pair-bonded to me without even courting me first! There was no choice."

"You wish me to court you?" He seemed intrigued.

The brute totally missed the point, completely disregarding her accusation. Grinding her teeth in frustration, Claire buried her head against his chest and tried to pretend Shepherd was not there, that his cock was not growing flaccid inside her, and that the damned hum was not in her chest.

***

It was three days later, at least, she thought it was three days, when Claire woke up to find a large sketchpad, two brushes, and a set of watercolors resting innocently on the bedside table. The new things were like a magnet. She rolled out of bed and snatched them up greedily. Yesterday's dress was pulled over her head, and within minutes, she was on her belly, legs kicking behind her, the paints mixed, and the beginnings of a view coming alive on the paper.

She spent hours rendering her favorite flowers, the red poppies that bloomed in the Gallery Gardens, drenching them in sunshine under a blue, dome-free sky.

"Your talent is greater than I imagined."

Just about jumping out of her skin, Claire looked over her shoulder, pressed a hand to her heart, and shrieked, "How long have you been there?"

"Long enough," Shepherd answered, already crouched at her side.

Nervous, she scooped up her paints and brushes before the giant stepped on them or got in a mood and took them away. Everything was cleaned in the bathroom sink. When she was done, Shepherd sat on the bed, his elbows resting on his knees, the drying artwork leaning against the wall by the bedside table.

"What time is it?" Claire asked, closing the bathroom door behind her.

He was hunched over, staring at the painting, a strange look in his eye. "The sun is rising."

Edging nearer the display, she reached out a hand to center her work. When she glanced toward the resting behemoth, she found his eyes held a trace of amusement, as if he found her behavior endearing.

Claire took a step back.

"You were going to smile," he grunted, as if he expected her to do so on command.

Green eyes, almost the same shade as the stems of the poppies, turned back to the painting. She knew it made no difference whether she smiled or not. "If I smiled now, I wouldn't mean it."

"You do not like your gifts?"

Hands fisted in the stuff of her skirt, she nodded. "I like the paints. You know that."

Standing, Shepherd moved toward his desk. "Paint another one."

Claire didn't paint, that mood had passed.

Sitting like an overgrown hulk at the small desk, Shepherd accessed his COMscreen and ignored her. Claire began her ritual pacing, a caged animal denied the room to run. Darting a glance at the back of his hated head, she suspected his inattention was some ruse. That, at any moment, he would turn around and pull out his cock.

But the exclusion continued—as if he were trying to break her down, confuse her... doing it subtly until she just cracked.

Breathing irregularly, her fists clenched in her hair, pulling black locks, she repeated over and over inside her skull. "I am Claire."

"Come here." The order was issued in a moderate voice, Shepherd having not even turned his head in her direction.

The last time she ignored a summons, he'd fucked her three times in a row, even as she begged him to stop—left her spent and replete until she could do nothing but lie still and stare at the wall. Moving to stand at his side, her hair wild, Claire did as she was told.

A large hand enveloped the entirety of her hip, pulling her a few inches closer before the mountain turned. "Your brooding is making you upset."

Why was she being reprimanded for having feelings? Normal humans who were not psychopathic murderers had feelings. And normal people did not do well for weeks on end in the same fucking room with only a monster for company!

Working his massive thumb into the hollow below her hip bone, Shepherd took in her disturbed expression. "Sing something for me."

"Uhhh…" What? Sing? Claire did not want to mate, and that was the probable outcome if she refused. Scowling, she rubbed her lips together and tried to slow down her thoughts long enough to think of a song. Nothing came to mind. "What kind of song?"

"Something soothing."

He was trying to get her to self-soothe. Well, he could go fuck himself. After a minute or two of deliberation, with the same steady pressure of his thumb moving against her skin, Claire settled on a well-known ballad older than the time of the domes. It was sappy and portrayed romance in a totally untrue light, but she had always liked it.

Though now she knew better. There was no such thing as true love—of that Claire was certain—only indoctrination, chemicals, and bastards who kept you locked in rooms.

By the time she neared the end, her voice had grown desolate. The brooding had been replaced with despair. There was never going to be a hero. The growing cord of the bond made it clear that she would only ever have the large Alpha seated before her. A man whose face she hated with her whole heart.

"Kneel."

The pressure of Shepherd's hand gently suggested she follow the order on her own, or he would press her down. Degraded, she went to her knees and looked up into his silver eyes, her lower lip trembling, certain he would punish her for thinking such dark thoughts.

When all he did was take her head and put it in his lap, she breathed out in relief. He petted her as he worked, Claire silently crying onto the fabric at his thigh, confoundedly comforted as he played with her hair.

There was a knock at the door. Surprised, she moved to get up. With a hand on the back of her neck, Shepherd kept her as she was, barking for the caller to enter. She should have known... it was all just a show for when his Follower came to call.

Since estrous had ruined her, no one had been in the room, no one had seen what she had become. Peeking for just a second, she saw the same Beta from the first day. The men spoke in a coarse language that meant nothing to her, Claire's face pressed against Shepherd's thigh.

The meeting extended until her knees began to ache, that weight ruffling the hair at the back of her skull never giving an inch. Placing her hand at Shepherd's thigh, she scratched gently to get his attention, aware that if she pushed away, he would retaliate—especially as another male was watching.

"Shepherd," Claire whispered his name against his leg, intruding in the men's conversation.

It had worked. The hand on her skull stroked down and lifted her chin until their eyes met. "Yes, little one?"

He looked clinically focused, and she was unsure if interrupting had been such a good idea. "My knees—"

Shepherd simply pulled her up to his lap and began absently rubbing her kneecaps, continuing the conversation with his officer as if it were nothing. Her face flaming, Claire was unsure which was worse:

kneeling at his feet like a dog, or being forced to sit on his lap like a child. If either man noticed her discomfort, it was not addressed.

The Omega looked to the Beta, measured his stiff posture and unsmiling face, noting how his attention never darted her way. He was much smaller than Shepherd, hardly taller than her, but seemed to have a whipcord quality to him that made Claire suspect he was very dangerous.

The meeting drew to a conclusion, and for a split-second, the man's vibrant baby-blues flicked toward her.

Shepherd growled so aggressively Claire jumped. The Follower bowed, a submissive stance, and left without another word.

Already pawing at her, turning her startled face toward his, Shepherd forced his Omega to meet flared iron eyes. She saw intense possession, the kind that made her stomach knot. Those hands, so large, began to rub, arranging her just as he wanted— stroking a breast, his scarring mark on her shoulder, circling her neck.

"Why were you looking at him?" It was spoken lowly, heavily laced with disapproval.

Claire answered, a line growing between her brows. "I have not seen anyone else in... I don't even know how long I have been locked in here."

"So you find it acceptable to openly stare at other males?"

Her scowl deepened, her voice confused. "Yes..."

Shepherd barked, his scarred lips snarling, "Your behavior is unacceptable. I gave you paints; you didn't thank me. I gave you comfort; you stared at the Beta."

Claire snapped. "I don't want fucking paints! I don't want to bow at your feet and be held like a pet on your lap. I want to go home! I want my life back!"

Angry, he shoved her off his thigh, letting her topple to the floor. Landing on her hip, she looked up, big eyes wide in her pale face. Everything in the cord between them was jostled badly... worse than her bones from the fall. The mountain was furious, slowly rising to his feet before her.

He looked about ready to crush her and she closed her eyes tight, anticipating the blow, welcoming an end to it all. There was silence, only the sound of her labored breath. Ten seconds passed and no move was made. When she finally cracked open an eye, Claire found she was alone. Shepherd had left her so soundlessly that not even the creaking door had dared whine.

Letting out a puff of air, she sagged back against the floor, her heart hammering away. It hit her then... there had been no slide of a metallic bolt shutting her in.

The door might be unlocked.

Panicked, totally shaken by the look of murder in her mate's eyes—not mate, she reminded herself—Shepherd's eyes. She stood and ran for the exit. Pulling the lever, it mercifully turned, and an empty hallway was right there before her.

Left or right? She didn't know the way, but she smelled Shepherd's scent clearly in one direction and bolted like a frightened rabbit down the opposite path. Before the city fell, she had run often around Thólos' many parks; not just for exercise, but to ensure she would be faster than any who might try to catch her. The weeks of lockup had done little to her speed. She ignored the painful thud of her bare feet against the floors. Tears were streaming down her cheeks, her breath ragged as she tried to keep inhalations to a runner's steady rhythm. Twisting and turning, she followed the sound of water. She found a ladder and flew up the rungs, oblivious to the sound of men's shouting voices, unaware of the dash of Followers trailing behind her. She flipped a hatch, eyes blinded by her first glimpse of bright sunlight in weeks, and scrambled out of the darkness.

She darted down a random causeway, winding in and out of alleys, climbing to higher terraces, her body steaming in the chilled lower region's weather. She came to a crossroads, heaved, and spat bile on the ground. Before her sat a broken bridge between two quarters, a massive, unscalable gap separating her from the nearest escape. The temptation to jump and end it all was so tempting. No more Thólos, no more Shepherd, no more falling into rapturous pieces when he fucked her, then hating herself afterwards.

But there were still the other Omegas... and she had let them down. They needed to know about the little blue pills, needed to know that Shepherd would not help them. It was that feeling alone that moved her feet again.

Claire ran for miles, ran in a crazy pattern that would make no sense to any who could smell her, ran until she vomited and fell in a pile against iron girders. Then she saw him, and he might have just been the most beautiful thing her eyes had ever beheld. A Beta, a stranger, was reaching down to help her... leading her sobbing body away from all the cold and pain.

He told her his name was Corday.

Chapter 4

Claire woke on an unfamiliar couch with actual sun on her face. Head aching, she sat up and looked around. The Beta's one room accommodation was small, sparse like hers, with little more than necessities and only a single, wilted, air-scrubber plant.

Corday himself was standing in the kitchen, frying eggs from the smell of it.

"Do you like coffee, miss?"

God, she had not had access to coffee in months. Already salivating, she nodded, her green eyes so wide it made him chuckle. The young man walked over with a lopsided grin, handing her a plate and the steaming beverage. "Sorry, I don't have sugar or milk."

She couldn't care less. The mug went to her lips, Claire sipping with a contented sigh. "Thank you."

"Just eat up. When you're finished, you can shower and—not to make this awkward—but you might want to put on some of my dirty clothes to mask your scent."

After all the running, all the sweat, she reeked of Omega. His offer was extraordinarily kind, assuming he was not just cornering her like the last man had.

Reading the troubled look on the woman's face, Corday added, "I'm not going to hurt you."

Suspicious, she asked, "Why are you helping me?"

"I'm an Enforcer."

She shook her head. "All the Enforcers are dead. I saw the Interdome Broadcast, the security footage at the gates of Judicial Sector. Shepherd's contagion killed them."

There was little Dome-humans feared more than the disease that had reduced billions down to a few million in one generation. That had forced skirmishes for supplies. The Red Consumption had destroyed global culture and left life safe only under the careful management of the Domes. Knowing Thólossens had seen his brothers and sisters-in-arms die coughing up blood, knowing that a pile of unconsecrated corpses waited in a section under lockdown, knowing potential Judicial Sector survivors would have been burned alive once quarantine procedure began, drained his smile away. Corday grew sad, his face suddenly seeming so very young. "Not all of us, miss. Some were on patrol outside the Judicial Sector before quarantine lockdown."

Her lower lip started to tremble. "My name is Claire."

"Are you okay, Claire?" Corday asked carefully, looking at a woman who showed all the reactive signs of abuse.

God, it was so nice to hear someone say her name. Whispering, she shook her head, "I'm not okay."

Skirting the couch, he sat as far from the shaken woman as the sofa would allow. With his hands on his knees and brown eyes soft, he suggested, "Tell me what happened to you."

She knew that the second she said the name Shepherd, Corday would kick her ass out on the street. She hated to lie, but she needed a shower and warm clothing to survive in the Lower Reaches.

But maybe she didn't have to lie. Maybe all she needed to do was start at the beginning. "The chem pushers are selling counterfeit heat-suppressants. They look just like the little blue pills... but they are not heat-suppressants. They're fertility drugs. They cause us to go into estrous unexpectedly, where we are unprepared and exposed."

"And this happened to you?" Corday asked, gently urging her to continue.

Claire didn't say yes or no, she didn't have to. The huge tears dripping down her cheeks were answer enough.

Realizing she was close to falling to pieces, Corday nodded and promised, "I'll look into it. Now finish your lunch." His boyish grin returned, and he backed off to return to his stove, teasing, "I had to fight six Alpha females to get those eggs."

She forced a laugh at the joke, the coffee going back to her lips. But it was hard to enjoy. The unshakable paranoia that Shepherd would burst through the door at any moment made her stomach churn. Or worse yet, Corday could be lying, waiting for an Alpha he could sell her to.

With her mind running in circles, she watched the young man. There was no projection of attraction. He was not sexually aroused. He was just a guy cooking eggs in his kitchen. He seemed genuine and harmless... he even smelled acceptable. But no one in Thólos could be trusted, not after the breach had unleashed chaos and the citizens became like animals.

The invaders had just come from the ground like ants—spewing from the Undercroft, from sentences for crimes deemed inexcusable—all of it so precise that Thólos' government fell within hours. All of it easy because the population was terrified of the transmission which looped on Interdome Broadcast.

Everyone watched accelerated signs of Red Contagion, the symptoms of that great plague known even to the youngest, decimate the very men and women sworn to protect Thólos citizens.

Shepherd threatened to infect them all should any resist.

The city turned on each other. Once peaceful men and women dragged anyone they found questionable to the Citadel to be disposed of. And there she was, forcing cold eggs down her throat, terrified Corday would turn on her.

She didn't approach him to give back the plate, just set it at the edge of his counter before scampering toward the lavatory to bathe. Under unheated water, Claire scrubbed every bit of Shepherd off of her body, knowing Corday had smelled the Alpha scent she was saturated in... mortified the little string in her chest seemed to twang as if pulled taut by a demanding pair-bond.

59

She closed her eyes and could practically hear Shepherd raging, his angry breath coming in long roars. Then something far more disturbing ran under her skin. If she felt his fury, he felt her abject terror. Because of the tie, Shepherd was still with her, there even at that moment in the shower, sensing her though the link. Hyperventilating, Claire mentally repeated, only instincts, and forced her eyes open to prove that nothing but discolored tiles surrounded her.

Shepherd wasn't there. He wasn't watching her, ready to rip out her throat.

Turning off the spray, Claire dried with a towel saturated in another man's scent—a man who had not once tried to hurt her... at least not yet. From his laundry, she pulled out the most pungent pieces, dressing in a sweater he must have exercised in and a pair of sweatpants that, knowing guys, probably had not been washed in weeks.

Standing at the mirror, she found queer green eyes in the reflection and wished she understood why the face looking back at her was filled with regret. Disgusted with that woman, Claire spun around and returned to the living room. Corday was still standing in the kitchen, eating his own meal. He nodded, his mouth full.

"I have no way to barter or repay you for the clothes right now, but when I can, I will." Her voice sounded nothing like her, it was the voice of a stranger.

When Corday saw her move toward the door, he swallowed quickly and approached with caution. "Ma'am, you're in shock. I don't think it's a good idea for you to be wandering the Dome. What you need is to rest, get your bearings. You will be safe here, if you need a place to regroup."

Everything he said seemed so sensible, even the weight of his hand on her shoulder, steering her back to the couch. Mechanically, Claire lay down. He covered her with a blanket and sleep hit her hard, a corner of her mind still marveling at the feeling of sun on her face.

***

Bad dreams began that very first night. Claire was running through Thólos, through smoke and evil. The buildings she climbed were ruins, many burning. Everything was decimated, just like the photos of Pre-Reformation War cities on visual in the Archives. No matter which direction she turned, she could not escape the mob at her back. The jeering faces of raging Alphas, violent Betas... they wanted to rip her to pieces because everything was her fault. She had sent the monster into a rage. She was the reason Thólos would know even more suffering.

Hands began to grip her clothes but she pressed forward, lungs burning as she tried to find any path through the smoke. She took a wrong turn, found herself trapped atop a broken viaduct, hounded and petrified. But then he was there in the darkness, waiting for her. Standing like a mountain, Shepherd reached out, beckoning her to him with the flick of his fingers.

With the dogs at her back and the devil before her, she did not know where to turn. All she could do was jump to her death.

Claire woke screaming.

Corday rushed from his bed, clicking on a torch to offer something besides the enforced dark of Thólos curfew.

"It's okay. You're safe, Claire." His voice came out soothing.

She threw her arms around the stranger and held on for dear life. "He'll find me here," she whispered, trembling. "He's already looking."

"He won't find you here. Do you understand? It was just a bad dream. Whoever he was cannot force you anymore. You're free, you get to choose."

I get to choose?

The words resonated, and she began to calm. Leaning back, wiping the snot and tears from her face, Claire fought to pull it together.

Illuminated by the small light, Corday asked, "Would you like me to sit up with you?"

Shaking her head, she answered in an unsteady voice, "No... I feel better now. Thank you."

She was lying, of course.

There was no more sleep that night. She simply sat on the couch and started at shadows. It was only when the sun came up, when she could feel the light, that Claire found the courage to shut her eyes.

**

Corday left a note on the coffee table notifying the sleeping girl that he'd gone to garner provisions. With so many dead, it did not take long to find forgotten shoes for feminine feet in a closet where neighbors dwelled no longer.

On the causeways, Shepherd's Followers marched, hyper-vigilant. Corday made sure to keep his head down, to bypass all screening. Several people were pulled aside at random. That was nothing new, but that day Shepherd's men seemed only to target women—pulling off scarves, exposing covered hair, sniffing them up close. A few Alpha females grew riled. As it continued, even Betas began to show their teeth.

Messing with women was a sure way to start another round of riots. The females alone, Alphas especially, would react instinctively. If their children were near, they might be even more aggressive. Then there were their mates. Alpha or Beta, no one liked to see their woman harassed.

The air was tense as he passed by mob after mob. Corday was eager to return to the skittish Omega with his freshly gathered supplies.

She was awake, her head turning toward the door the instant she heard his key in the lock. When it was only the Enforcer offering a calming smile, Claire let out a breath and shook her head, as if she felt her reaction had been foolish.

63

Showing his worn catch, Corday said, "I found some shoes that might fit you."

"Those aren't very pretty," she tried to banter, but her voice came out flat, and what should have been funny was unnerving. Claire tried again, forcing inflection and a smile. "Thank you."

"It's Thursday. The power will be on in this zone tonight." He locked the door and set the shoes on the floor near the woman. "Rather than just watching the paint peel, I have a collection of old films. If you like, we can watch one."

"Okay."

While Claire pulled the new shoes over borrowed, stinking socks, Corday took a seat at the far end of the couch, the pair of them like mismatched bookends. He lifted the remote. When the screen came to life, all that played was the Thólos Interdome Broadcast. Unfamiliar correspondents looped every five minutes, detailing which sectors would receive fresh rations the following day, locations of supply pick up points, faces of wanted criminals.

Claire heard nothing, the entirety of her attention was on the date stamped at the corner of the screen. "Five weeks..."

Corday didn't need to be a genius to grasp what the woman had muttered. Five weeks, that was how long she'd been trapped.

She was trying to hide her horror, so Corday inserted the stick that held his precious films and chose something lighthearted most people would recognize. It worked. Thirty minutes in and Claire's shoulders lost their rigidness.

"I used to watch this with my dad when I was a kid," she offered, glancing at him with a small, half-felt smirk. "He loved this movie."

Corday gave her a crooked grin. "Your dad sounds like he has excellent taste."

"He did," Claire agreed, her face less tragic. "He was a really funny guy. Sooo Alpha, though."

They both snickered, knowing exactly what that meant. Alpha parents were fanatical about their children. Over-involved, bragging constantly... generally an embarrassing pain in the ass.

"What about your mom?"

"An uptight Omega with no sense of humor... she left when I was twelve."

That was very unusual. Children typically made Omegas incredibly dedicated parents. Besides, the pair-bond would have compelled her to return to her Alpha. Corday wanted to ask, it was all over his face, so Claire just spit it out—it was old news, after all. "She found a quiet place near the Gallery Gardens and took a bottle of pills—overdosed. She couldn't stand a life tied to someone she didn't like."

"I'm sorry."

Shaking her head, her dark hair swaying, Claire said, "Don't be. In the end, she got her choice. I respect that." Looking back to the screen, she asked, "What about you? What are your parents like?"

"Both Betas. Dad was sent to the Undercroft when I was a kid. He, uh, stole things. Mom raised me. She died the day Thólos was breached."

Green eyes looked back at the man on the couch, at the one who had been kind to her. The lines between his brows spoke of grief. "I'm sorry."

There seemed to be an understanding between them. "Me too."

Both looked back to the projection, laughing at all the right parts, neither one-hundred percent sure if the other was faking. When the credits rolled, Corday made them dinner, surprised to find the kitchen had been scrubbed clean in his absence. He watched the back of her head, saw her nervously play with her hair, and wondered how on earth the world had become what it was.

**

If Claire sat on the floor just right and angled her head, there was a thin patch of sky the surrounding structures did not block. Direct, delicious sun warmed her skin, but something in all of it was hollow. Corday had not told her to leave, and she had to admit she was terrified of even stepping outside. It seemed so ironic that all she had wanted was to breathe fresh air, and now that she could... she could not. But she could look out that window, crouched down low so not a soul but the birds flying overhead could see her.

Eyes on the clouds, Claire felt her mind slowly grow quiet, sighed deeply, and enjoyed the warm rumble of ambient noise. It took almost an hour before she was startled out of her daydream, to panic at a sound that shouldn't be there.

Shepherd's purr was all around her.

Certain that the behemoth was standing behind her, her head flew around, her eyes frantically searching the small studio apartment. No one was there.

But he was...

Claire knew—logically—she was alone, but she could practically smell him in the air. Heart racing, she pulled her knees under her chin and went back to her view, determined to control her mind. The harder she fought, the warmer the worm in her chest grew. Over and over, a soft little tug came to the thread. It was the strangest sensation, as if the beast was utterly calm now, calling to her almost gently.

Claire didn't trust it for a second.

Shepherd was an aggressive man—in conversation, in behavior, in bed. There was no 'gentle' unless it served him. And the kindness she'd received was always calculating. He had no feelings—or if he did, they were so twisted up in megalomania they didn't really count. Whatever he thought he might gain by trying to lure her with something as elusive as a soft invitation through the bond, she was not going to comply. Claire was going to keep that window and that little slice of sky, rejecting darkness and isolation.

A few hours later, she was back on the couch, reading a book she had pulled from Corday's small collection. It was the first time her eyes had met paper in ages. Underground, she had never once touched Shepherd's books—as if his forbidden texts might infect her with his warped view and evil.

It felt good to do something normal.

At dusk, Corday returned. They exchanged customary pleasantries, Claire waiting for him to show her the door. Once again, he seemed unconcerned that an interloper was sitting quietly in his apartment's only room. Corday attended to his own things, she went back to the book, and before she knew it, the lights were out and she was lying back on the couch, prepared to face a night awake in the terrifying dark.

Should she sleep, vivid dreams plagued and tormented—the same scene over and over. In every nightmare, Shepherd lurked in the dark, violent strangers' hands reaching to grasp and hurt her if she didn't run toward him, if she didn't climb higher up the wrecked tower.

The viaduct that could carry her to a better zone, the thing she had raced toward—it was always broken. There was no escape. To her left stood her great nightmare, to her right, blurred faces of the ones eager to watch her bleed. She could feel it in that towering damaged causeway; the icy air rushing up from the lower reaches, the sweat on her face from the run. Then there were the mercurial eyes. Steady eyes. Determined eyes.

From the shadows, Shepherd would reach out a hand to her, silent in the din of wrathful screams, and crook his fingers. To Claire's horror, each night her feet moved one step closer to the thing she feared most.

She would wake in a cold sweat, surging from the couch just to make sure Corday was there. Fortunately, the Beta slept like the dead, snoring just a little. It was a sound that brought her great comfort. Whispering so she would not wake him, she talked to herself, explaining her fear wasn't real. Dreams were nothing more than the influence of the pair bond.

She was free. She got to choose.

When the urge to vomit passed and the fevered trembling ended, Claire would lie back and try to think of nice things. Every night, as she stared at Corday's ceiling, the boy's snores eventually turned into the sound of far more masculine breaths the moment sleep came upon her again. The sensation of a warm hand stroking her hair to soothe her, her unconscious desire to hear only a moment of purrs... One small slip and the dream would invade again; a dozen times a night, a hundred? It felt like a never-ending loop.

The sun would rise and so would Claire, more tired than the day before. Corday noticed it too, she could tell by the way he darted subtle glances at her, how he skirted the walls and made sure not to get too close. Neither of them spoke of her degradation. After all, what was the point? It was not until the fifth day—when Corday told her that he would not be back until morning—that the Beta reached into his pocket and pulled out a circular, white pill.

"This will help you sleep, if you want it."

With a conciliatory smile, he left it on the counter and wished her a good day. Claire didn't touch it, found herself far too mesmerized by the round pharmaceutical and how much trouble they had turned out to be in her life. The temptation to drop it down the sink was as strong as the temptation to swallow it immediately.

All day that little pill stared at her. Her fingers curled at the edge of the counter, Claire crouched down to be at eye-level with the little white temptation. What if she took it and sleep did come? What if the dream came with it, and she could not wake up to save herself from taking those final steps towards a man the manipulative pair-bond was twisting into a savior? What if she took a whole bottle of pills?

In the end, when the dark came, she did not take the little white pill. She hid it instead. Lying in the darkness, buried under heaps of blankets, Claire closed her eyes and the same movie played on repeat in her mind. Silver eyes, an outreached hand, villains and smoke... only that night, each time she woke there was no snoring anchor in the corner of the room for her to pace her heartbeats to. Curled up and delirious from days without rest, she felt she was going mad, hearing things, confused. As the hours stretched by, Claire realized with a creeping apprehension that it was Shepherd's raspy breath she kept imagining in the corner, not the Beta's snores,

Shepherd's hand she almost believed was stroking her hair.

She felt in her bones that if she could only hear a few moments of that purr, untroubled sleep would come at last.

Chapter 5

"Shepherd's genetic markers do not match any prisoner on record. I am telling you." Brigadier Dane was adamant. "He was not incarcerated in the Undercroft."

Corday had heard a thousand explanations. Not one of them was possible. Outside the Dome spread one hundred kilometers of frozen tundra in every direction, the location of Thólos chosen specifically so any potential diseased wanderers could never survive approach. Everything inside was self-sustaining, and only twice in his lifetime had shuttles been permitted to land. All on board had been female, citizens from other biospheres invited to Thólos Dome to keep the gene pool fresh.

Those who came never left, just as those who had left to serve the same duty on foreign soil would never return.

Scans for all new arrivals were vigorous. There was no way any unexpected life-form could have passed the gates. Even so, the last exchange had been nearly a decade ago.

Voicing his opinion to the few Enforcer stragglers gathered in secret, Corday disagreed. "The man is covered in Da'rin markings. He was branded by the gangs in the Undercroft and labored down there long enough to organize outcasts into an army, to have constructed numerous tunnels that had gone unnoticed all throughout Thólos."

Brigadier Dane was not exactly a fan of Recruit Corday. Her patience with the young man was slender. "Then explain why he doesn't exist on record."

Corruption was a disease even the Dome could not filter out. Jaw rigid, Corday said, "Because someone threw him down there off record."

"If that was the case, others would have known. You can't just march down those tunnels dragging a man behind you. The security protocols alone would have been logged. If a soul had gone missing, people would have noticed. What you suggest would require a conspiracy of epic proportions."

There was one man in the room who had the power and the clearance to know. Several sets of eyes turned to Senator Kantor, all of them demanding he confirm that no such atrocity was possible.

The old man raised a hand to silence petty arguments. "I'd like to say it isn't possible, but I can't. Just as it should not have been possible for those trapped in the Undercroft to emerge, for our government to fall, or for our people to have gone mad. There is much about the insurgency we don't know. At this point, the identity of the Followers' fanatical leader is less important than discovering where he has stored the contagion."

Speaking because nothing made sense, Corday sighed. "Brigadier Dane's intel would explain Shepherd's attack on the Senate and why he's hung the corpses from the Citadel. It might be an act of revenge."

73

Brigadier Dane narrowed her eyes. "Or just the act of a psychopath..."

Twenty-seven bodies in various stages of decomposition polluted the filtered air with stink. Men and women who had served the Dome, chosen by the people, swung in the updrafts.

Then there was the one name no one dared mention. Even after all those months, there was still a complete lack of information on missing Premier Callas—the unelected head of the Thólos government. All that was known was that the Premier's sector had been locked down in the first moments of the breach, a steel barricade cutting his residence off from the rest of the Dome. Shepherd's Followers ignored it, citizens no longer kept vigil there begging for sanctuary, it was just another shut gate with gods only knew what on the other side.

Brigadier Dane had more to say, the female looking to the last subordinate she expected would actually support her theory—to Corday, her expression distrustful. "But it doesn't explain how he came to be armed with the Red Consumption, or how the disease was smuggled into Thólos."

Grey hair shaggy without the clean trim he'd sported in office, Senator Kantor shook his head. It seemed hard for the old man to speak, to formulate exactly how he was to explain. "Before the doors were sealed, several strains of Red Consumption had been collected for study, the secret of its keeping only accessible to the highest tier of government. Thirty-four years ago, there was an accident in the lab which had been charged with creating a vaccine. The strain had aggressively mutated. A tech was infected. In a matter of minutes, the entire lab was locked under quarantine." Senator Kantor seemed utterly sad, as if reliving the memory of something truly unspeakable. "I watched the security feed. Incineration protocol failed. The souls locked behind the gates, they suffered... before they died."

Horror sat on the faces of those huddled in the dark, the group speechless.

Swallowing, trying to wrap his head around the fact that the very plague which had ripped apart humanity had been knowingly stored inside the Dome, Corday breathed, "And the mutated strain... how did it get out of the lab? How did it get into Shepherd's hands?"

Frowning, Senator Kantor replied, "I don't know. The lab is off the grid, sealed. Even I never knew where it was."

If one of the most powerful men in the Senate lacked that knowledge, and with the majority of his colleagues dead or missing, this new information left the ragged Enforcers with nothing but more questions that could not be answered.

Seeing so many struggling men and women consumed with even greater doubt left Senator Kantor squaring his shoulders and taking on the tone of an orator. "Friends, there is still much we do not know, and speculation without fact to support us will only breed argument. We go one step at a time, and trust the gods will lead us to salvation."

Face grim, shaken like the others, Corday offered a worthy, immediate goal the group might sink their teeth into. "I know where we can begin. I have learned that the chem pushers working the causeways are selling fake heat-suppressants. Omegas in hiding are going into estrous while unprepared and most likely exposed. They are being brutalized."

Senator Kantor frowned, seizing on to the offered duty. "Where did you hear of such things?"

Looking at the Alpha, Corday tried not to let his lingering disgust show in his expression. "A few days ago, I came across a very frightened Omega female, collapsed mid-deck."

Brigadier Dane eased a step closer, an intrigued arch in her brow. "What did she look like?"

Corday shrugged his shoulders. "What's that matter?"

"It matters," Senator Kantor explained in a level voice, pulling a leaflet from his pocket, "because there is a very large bounty out on this woman."

It was a flyer, similar to every other wanted sign littering the Dome. The young woman was smiling, her waving black hair tousled as if by an updraft, her green eyes sparkling, gentle and inviting. Claire O'Donnell looked lovely and vibrant... and though the version Corday had met was shattered and frightened, she was the Omega who was sleeping on his couch.

It all started making sense. The women were being harassed in the food lines because everyone was looking for her. And the bounty itself was a king's ransom. "What's she wanted for?"

Senator Kantor's lips went into a line and he shook his head. "I don't know, but she may have information valuable to our cause."

Corday could not take his eyes off the photo. He took a deep breath, let it out of his nose, and muttered, "Then you better come to my apartment." Glancing at the Senator, he added, "But you must understand, she is not going to be comfortable around an Alpha right now. And if you show her that leaflet, it might just send her over the edge."

Senator Kantor was already walking towards the exit. "The rest of you are dismissed. Corday, you will take me to her immediately."

***

It was almost dawn when she heard the key in the door. After a night of hellish sleep and total exhaustion, Claire was jumpy, bolting towards the wall when another man—an Alpha—came into the room behind Corday.

"Don't come near me!" she snarled, looking for anything she could use to strike him with. Settling on a lamp, she clutched it so hard it shook.

Senator Kantor and Corday waited by the door so Claire might feel a bit less cornered.

The older Alpha exercised the kindest voice, soft soothing eyes, and years of experience playing to a crowd. "Do you know who I am?"

With lips pressed in a line and eyes narrowed to slits, she nodded. "You're Senator Kantor." The man known as Champion of the People; beloved by many for his outreach to the proletariat, laboring for the greater good in the Lower Reaches.

"I am not here to hurt you." He cocked his head at the young Enforcer. "Corday says you need help. I'd like to see what I can do."

Her sweaty grip tightened on the lamp. "I don't want you coming any closer."

"I can stay over here." He smiled softly, even backing up a few steps to sit on a stool by the kitchen counter.

It seemed to appease the Omega, and she slowly lowered the makeshift weapon. From the dark smudges under her eyes, Corday could tell she had hardly slept, could smell the lingering tinge of fear in the air. There was a standoff, Claire silent as she watched the Alpha like a hawk. Senator Kantor waiting, letting her do what she felt she needed to.

When several minutes had passed and her chest stopped heaving, the old man began. "You were taking the counterfeit heat-suppressants and went into estrous in a place that was dangerous."

"Yes."

"What happened?"

Rubbing her lips together, she took a deep breath. "What matters... the only way you can help me is to find a way to protect the hidden Omegas. They are starving... they need food."

"I need to know what happened to you before I can figure out how to help you all."

Her back was pressed so sharply against the wall, Claire's shoulder blades dug into it. With an expression that grew positively wretched, she fought to say, "It was dangerous to take our share at the designated areas. More of us were getting picked off every day, and those of us who did get food... it was never enough to feed us all. So it was decided that I would go to the Citadel to ask in person for help.

"I was taking the pills, covered in clothing that had been on a rotting corpse to mask my scent. I climbed the steps and found him. He would not acknowledge me, so I waited." She drew a shaky breath and stopped.

Corday picked up for her, saying cautiously, "And you went into heat in the Citadel..."

Claire nodded.

The young man continued, "And someone took advantage."

She tried to explain, but she just could not get that name past her tongue. "There was a riot. He killed a lot of people and carried me off."

Both men noticed that she had not once said Shepherd—that she continued to refer to Shepherd as him. It was Senator Kantor who posed the question as delicately as he could. "And Shepherd was the one who took you?"

Claire began to cry, whimpering as she fell to pieces. "He refused to give us our share. Instead he demanded I tell him where the Omegas were so they could be taken and used by his men. He forced a pair-bond... kept me locked in his room for weeks." Her hand went to her chest, her fist knocking against it. "And I can still feel him, right here."

They were stunned, both slack-jawed.

A pair-bond... the man was searching for his mate.

Corday shook his head as if it were impossible. He could understand why a villain like Shepherd would rut her through a heat, but to actually pair-bond with a stranger seemed extreme. A bond was forever. There was no known way to break it without the death of one of the pair. And the aftermath was messy—oftentimes the living partner could never pair again. He'd taken Claire for life. No wonder she was so terrified. A man with the power to take over an entire colony, with devoted Followers at his back, was hunting her down and bonded to her.

She opened her eyes and forced herself to stop crying. "I have to tell the Omegas. I have to go to them."

All Corday could mumble was, "You can't go outside, Claire. This is Shepherd we are talking about. His influence under the Dome is almost absolute."

"I can't abandon them. I should have gone sooner, but I..." She didn't need to say she was afraid, that fact was obvious.

"You are a very brave woman." In a voice encouraging and strong, Senator Kantor spoke his piece. "What you tried to do for the others was incredibly courageous, but you cannot do it alone. Let us assist you. Together we'll find a way to help the Omegas."

"How?" Large green eyes went to the soft-spoken older man.

"For now, we'll get them food, proper pharmaceuticals... but there will need to be a long-term solution. How many are there?"

Shaking her head, she wiped her eyes. "There were around eighty-five the last time I saw them. But it's been over a month, it could be half that number... I have no idea."

"Where are they?" Senator Kantor asked.

Her face grew instantly hard and threatening. Claire straightened her spine and said nothing. She would speak to the Omegas first, they would decide before she revealed the location to anyone. Period.

The woman's challenging expression was not missed. Senator Kantor raised a hand and added, "I mean them no harm."

She growled, a bit of her old spirit coming through. "I don't trust any Alpha."

"I understand." And he did. It would be impossible to expect a woman who had been through what she had experienced to expose others to the same potential fate.

"Give me a few days to consider all options, to get some food together as well." Senator Kantor stood from his stool, Claire already lifting the lamp again in warning. The Senator nodded a goodbye, and left.

The day passed in silence between Corday and Claire, but that night, they watched another film together on opposite ends of the couch, a bowl of popcorn in the middle. Knowing her penchant for comedy, Corday had chosen his favorite, and it seemed to peel away the suspicious attitude that had made Claire restlessly pace all through the day.

When it was time for bed, she seemed settled and Corday went to sleep certain she was stronger than she had been before.

She was.

Once Claire heard his snores, she climbed silently from the couch, stole his coat, and left to find the Omegas. It was dark, the tower lights snuffed, Shepherd's manipulation of the power grid enforcing curfew. Memorizing where she was so she could find her way back to the rambling structure, Claire ran— from shadow to shadow—all the way to a squalid site caught between zones: a frost-covered scrapyard on the lowest level, where every breath came out like fog.

The forgotten dump had been filled, abandoned, and shut up before she'd been born. Nobody went there, and the government had never re-purposed the site. Like all things deemed unclean, and due to the fact it was in the frigid Lower Reaches, the area was generally avoided. It was perfect for the Omegas: shelter to sleep in, enough water in the air that it could be collected and drunk without having to draw water in the upper levels and carry it down. But it was an icebox. They had no power and no heat.

"It's Claire!" A shout went up once the black-haired girl made it through a crack in the wall, Claire staggering closer to the women crowded together for warmth.

Gulping for breath, she hung her head between her knees, trying to speak even though winded. "Blue pills, fake..."

Someone brought her water, a match was struck, and a precious candle lit. Huddled around the light was a sight that made Claire's heart ache. The Omegas were skeletal, and so many were looking at her with eyes totally devoid of hope. But with the light, expressions changed. Some bloomed at her arrival, others fell dark with suspicion. Worst of all was the flat out envy... and Claire understood the reason. Shepherd had been feeding her. She was healthy. She had been given food while they had had nothing.

It was Nona, one of the elders respected by the group, who spoke first. "Sweet goddess! Claire, I've been so worried."

Her green eyes looked upon the familiar heart-shaped face, half-hidden by lank salt and pepper hair. "How many are left?"

"Last head count was fifty-six."

Claire felt sick. Fifty-six... practically a third of the remaining Omegas had been picked off while she had been imprisoned by Shepherd. "I have so much to tell you." Her voice grew stronger. "If you have not already figured it out, the blue pills are not heat-suppressants... they are fertility drugs. I went into my cycle right in the middle of the damn Citadel."

Gasps of horror, too many staring with pity, shamed Claire.

"There's more. Shepherd will not help. He refuses to send rations and wanted me to disclose your location so that everyone could be taken, segregated from the population, and readied for his Followers."

"But isn't that what we want?" a redheaded woman by her side hissed.

Claire looked Lilian dead in the eye, saw the miserable state she'd been reduced to and said, "You would be imprisoned and offered to a stranger in estrous, bonded to a man of his choosing. He told me so himself."

"But would he feed us?"

"Is that what you want?" Her arched eyebrows went up. Claire wanted to rail, to berate the woman, but she did nothing more than shake her head and continue. "I have also met with Senator Kantor. He offers food. He wants to help us."

"How?" several voices asked in unison.

"He needs a few days to get a plan together. Once I find out what it is, I'll come back and tell you. Then we can all decide."

Nona put her hand on Claire's shoulder. "You are not going to stay? It's dangerous for you out there. Don't you know there is a huge bounty out on your head? Amelia saw the flyer two days ago."

Claire scowled, but the news was not exactly surprising.

Lilian poked the flesh of Claire's cheek. "You have grown fat. Shepherd's men were feeding you."

Brushing off the fingers, Claire barked, "I was trapped in a room for five weeks!"

"But they fed you!"

"Quiet, Lilian," Nona snapped at the instigator. "You're hungry, not stupid... you can tell from her altered scent that Claire has been pair-bonded. They would feed what they want to keep. Instead of remaining with her mate, she escaped and came here to help us all."

Claire was mortified.

Did she really smell different? When more eyes began to shine at her in the light of the candle and noses began to sniff, all she could do was try not to shrink back.

The question was tossed around. "Which one was it? Who claimed you?"

Answering quickly, Claire muttered, "It doesn't matter."

Lilian, her lips curled in a nasty sneer, laughed under her breath. Claire tried to remind herself that the redhead was starving to death, lived in a constant state of terror. Her feral behavior was understandable.

"I better go." Claire pulled Nona into a hug. "Expect me back in a few days."

It felt good to smell and hold someone so familiar, someone she knew cared about her. When the extended embrace came to an end, Claire left, climbing through the dark causeways of Thólos all the way up to Corday's apartment.

He'd never even known she'd been gone.

Chapter 6

With his head ducked low between his shoulders, Corday walked across the shadowed causeway, the man ahead in the flapping coat eyeing him like fresh meat.

For two days he'd watched the chem pusher peddle to so many citizens it seemed staggering how freely the drug rings operated now that the Enforcers were off the radar. The thug made absolutely no secret of his unlawful business, almost taunting whoever might challenge his actions to dare speak it to his face.

Without greeting, Corday grunted, "I need your heat-suppressants, the little blue ones."

"Sure thing, man." It was obvious, apparent in the tone and cadence of the chem pusher's speech, that the dealer was an Outcast. By the dilation of his pupils, one who sampled his own wares. Sagging jowls bouncing, he pulled out a bottle. "Gonna cost ya. Going rate's a kilo of fresh produce and five rations of meat."

"That right?" Corday shook his head, trying to avoid noticing any family resemblance in a convict the same age his father would have been. "I have something far more valuable than food we're willing to trade… if you can manage twenty or thirty bottles."

Yellowed eyes narrowed. "Why do you need so many?"

Corday gave the man the most perverted of grins. "Let's just say, we like to keep our Omegas begging for it. If you supply, you can partake."

"A man after my own heart." Chipped, brown teeth on display, a knowing smile accompanied the pusher's question, "How many did you catch?"

Corday shrugged. "Enough to keep half the zone's dicks wet, so long as they're locked in estrous."

Scratching his chin, the chem pusher cleared a great deal of phlegm from his throat laughing. "Shepherd's Followers slaughter any man caught with an induced Omega. A wise businessman might look for more than just meds…"

Voice disinterested, Corday asked, "Such as?"

"What you really came here for. Partners. My gang ain't afraid of Shepherd or his Followers. We can supply you and keep business running smooth."

Hearing Shepherd's name thrown about casually, brought a sneer to Corday's face. "Fuck Shepherd."

"Sky-breather... without men like us at your back, Shepherd will fuck you."

Cracking his neck, Corday muttered, "He doesn't scare me."

Breath which stank of rotting things slid like grease up Corday's nose, the thug leaning nearer to taunt, "That's cause you ain't never seen him kill, or watched psychos bow to kiss his feet."

Meeting those yellowed eyes, Corday stepped far too close for comfort. "You must think us sky-breathers are pretty stupid. The racket ain't nothing new. But, unlike you, we weren't dumb enough to get caught and crammed in the Undercroft. I said fuck Shepherd, and I meant it."

The man flat-out guffawed. "You're one cocky little motherfucker. If your stock is any good, I'll get you what you need, kid. As much as you need. And you'll get us exactly what we want. That's how an alliance works. Or do they call it a trade agreement under the Dome?"

***

"They really must think every last law-abiding Enforcer is gone," Brigadier Dane muttered under her breath.

The idiot on the causeways was either mentally challenged, or outright shameless of his crimes, acting as if consequence no longer existed. Not once had he suspected that Corday slipped a tracking device onto his person, not once had he even seemed wary. And even now that the creep was back in his cozy, dingy hole, she could hear the man laughing, the sounds of grunts, and hoarse, animalistic noises in the background.

It was hard to listen to. The Alpha female was fully aware of what was going on behind the concrete walls bad men thought would keep their flagrant secret safe.

What Corday had claimed to possess— Omegas kept like livestock—these men had in

89

quantity. And they were being used even as the thug from the causeway plotted with his chums just how he planned to slice up the cocky kid who had such a mouth, laughing at how easy it would be to double-cross the boy, and how much they would rake in offering something other than used, slack pussy to the men lining up outside.

Corday's continuous issue with insubordination aside, for once the Beta Enforcer had done something right. The atrocities committed against those females had to be stopped. All the men inside had to be wiped from existence. And order—even if it was only a small step back to the way things were before—had to be enforced.

Things had gone to hell under the Dome, the beauty of a functional system going up in smoke at the first sign of real trouble. It shamed Dane to see her brethren so weak, to know that the precious survivors of wars and plagues could still be reduced to nothing but the animals humanity had become before the Domes. Thólos Dome had been the bastion of civility. The greatest Dome on all the continents. What had been accomplished under the glass—the flourishing culture, the beauty of life beyond mere survival—was now abandoned by Erasmus Dome, by Bernard Dome, even by the poorest Vegra Dome. One hint of plague and any chance of support from the outside vanished.

The issue had to be solved internally. Shepherd and his Followers had to be removed. The contagion had to be destroyed. And the infection—men like the thugs Dane twitched to kill—purged. An example made for others to follow.

A day or two of surveillance and her team would demolish the upstart syndicate. Brigadier Dane smirked at the thought of a much-needed victory, eager to see the look on the wretches' faces when she shoved something unwelcome inside them—something pointy—to see how they liked it.

***

Claire was gaunt, blinking rapidly as she kept as far from Senator Kantor as the small space would allow. With Corday gone, the Senator had remained to question her in his absence, so they might discuss options for the Omegas.

The options, it seemed, were limited. But anything was preferable to the other outcome. Namely slavery, rape, or murder.

But help came at a price.

Senator Kantor was wise enough to keep his distance, to speak gently to the shifty-eyed woman pacing madly back and forth. "You must tell me about Shepherd. What you might know could save us."

Just hearing that name sent her attention to all the corners, as if the Alpha could be conjured with only a word. Stopping her feet, Claire wrung her hands. "I keep telling you, I can't. I don't know anything."

"You can do this," Senator Kantor urged. "Any information you divulge will help us all."

91

"You don't understand." Impatiently pushing her hair behind her ear, she tried her best not to trip up the words. "He didn't talk to me..."

The look of pity in Kantor's expression first inspired her anger, then shame. After what had happened, that look was one she would receive until the day she died.

The Alpha coaxed out the subtleties of what he needed. "We can just talk about the man, your observations."

"Okay..."

Senator Kantor started off simply. "The Da'rin markings, do you know what they are?"

Quoting what she'd been taught in school, Claire said, "Outcast tattoos—markings to depict whatever crime a prisoner was incarcerated for."

Nodding, Senator Kantor offered further insight, "Yet most are earned in the Undercroft, given from one inmate to another—a testament prisoners coax into patterns under the skin."

"Coax?"

"They are not made from ink. Da'rin is a parasite."

Brows drawn tight, Claire asked, "You purposefully infect convicts?"

"The men in the Undercroft live without sun, are exposed to difficult conditions. We subject them to a beneficial symbiotic relationship so they might tolerate the environment they labor in. And, should they escape, they are unable to hide amongst the general population. Not only because they are branded—you see, sunlight makes the marks burn."

But Shepherd openly wore his arms and neck displayed wherever he went, his large flexing muscles detailed with black for all to see. "That doesn't make sense."

The old man sighed. "The patterns Shepherd chose hold great meaning amongst outcasts. It could help the resistance if we had a better understanding of the man... if you could describe the images we have not seen, we might build a profile, learn his secrets."

Of course she knew Shepherd's marks by heart, could almost feel the heat of them moving under her roving palms. Face red, Claire stammered, "The ones on his arms, the ones you've seen. What are they?"

"A tally of the men he's killed."

Her embarrassed blush drained away, leaving her ashen. There were so many symbols swirled over the Alpha's flesh, hundreds of filigreed marks, thousands, and they extended over his chest, his back, his thighs and buttocks... even his...

Her fear came back stronger than before, the link buzzing as if to question why she remained scared and alone when her protector longed to care for her.

Senator Kantor stepped closer to regain her attention. "Is there anything you've seen amongst the tallies you might consider noteworthy?"

Just looking at the man, tears running down her face, Claire drew a blank. "He's covered, everywhere. The patterns mean nothing to me, just edges and swirls." All those times she'd traced fingertips over them in the dark, she'd been unknowingly admiring the death of another of Shepherd's victims. "I didn't know..."

The door opened, Corday returning to find Claire incredibly disturbed, her head in her hands.

"Claire." The Beta rushed forward. When she didn't panic, he drew her down to sit before her unsteady legs gave out. "You're safe here, remember? You don't need to be scared."

Something about Corday being in the room unhinged her tongue, Claire blurting out pointless observations in her horror over the marks. "His Followers speak another language. I never knew what they said." With a tired laugh that was disturbing in the extreme, she listed the only thing that was absolutely correct. "He likes to read. He holds my hair as he does it, so if I move, he'll know. I have to be very still."

Corday whispered the question, "What happened if you moved?"

"The book became less interesting." Claire quieted and turned her head towards the Senator, defiance drying her tears. "I was kept locked in a room. I had no exposure to anyone but him. There were no windows, everything was grey. The man never even shared a meal with me. Now, I've answered your questions, you answer mine. Beyond supplying true heat-suppressants, what will you do for the Omegas?"

The Senator, in dire need of a shave, offered a smile. "Once the numbers are assessed, separate cells of two or three will be smuggled to safe houses that can be defended and monitored."

Claire's ears pricked up, something in Kantor's statement sounding awfully familiar. "Why not just send food to where they are now? There is no need to move the group or break apart women who rely on one another for support."

"We can discuss that option, though I believe it leaves you far more vulnerable than entrusting them to our protection."

When had the government ever protected Omegas? Her kind practically had no rights without a mate to speak for them. "You will do nothing until I talk to the Omegas. They must decide," she said.

"Claire," Senator Kantor pleaded, stepping closer to the female who clearly had lost her faith. "You need to trust us and stay here where you are sheltered. We can approach your Omegas."

"No." Her voice sounded less like a frightened child and more like an angry woman. "I appreciate everything you offer, but even Shepherd couldn't drag the location of our hiding place from me. This plan you propose is their decision, and I will speak to them first."

"You haven't slept in days, you hardly eat..." Corday grew stubborn, squeezing her clammy fingers. "Wandering around Thólos in this state will get you killed. If you have to go, then take me with you. A Beta will be less threatening, and there is safety in numbers."

Taking her fingers from his hand, she considered. Coming to a decision was easy. "We'll go tonight, just you and me."

Both men seemed appeased.

Sheepish, Claire asked a favor. "I'm going to need clothing that can mask my scent. Everything here I have already worn... I cannot smell like an Omega."

Nodding that he understood, Corday went to his dresser and pulled on a heavy sweater. "I'll go for a run. You can wear these when I return."

Lashes lowering, she whispered, "Thank you."

Senator Kantor left, Corday his companion.

Alone, she stood from the sofa to prepare.

She needed a cold shower, all that freezing water would help clear the cobwebs. Claire cranked up the tap, eager for a deluge. She sighed the instant pipes groaned and her sleep-deprived mind mistook the noise for something very different. The effect was immediate. Under the spray, eyes closed, where there should only have been cold water streaming over her flesh, the heat of large hands replaced it.

Roughened palms flowed over the line of her spine, soothed the dip in her lower back... the air full of appreciative grunts. Those same hands, callused and familiar, stroked her soft belly, stole upward to hold the weight of her breasts, thumbs circling pert nipples until they were so sensitive Claire whimpered. The thread pulsed in her chest, generous slick dripping down her legs once the growl sounded a third time.

All around her, low breaths echoed deep and hungry, the heat of his chest pressed to her back, the thickness of his cock grinding at the cleft in her buttocks.

Two fingers were pushed into her mouth.

His order at her ear to suck, and Claire's eyes rolled back in her skull.

Pressed to the tile, nipples chafed by grout, Claire's tongue hungrily twisted as it was told to. The head of his cock, searing hot, prodded insistent where she ached. His was not a slow entry. Shepherd speared her, his rhythm erratic, filling the small enclosure with Claire's muffled cries no matter how he finger fucked her mouth.

Forehead against the tile, hardly able to breath, Claire came with a shriek. Everything inside her clenched, slick ran like a river, and the hallucination ended.

Phantom hands were gone.

There was no Shepherd.

No growls.

No licentious grunts.

All there had ever been was the sound of the pipes and her inadequate fingers working her pussy.

Shaken, she looked down at her hand, horrified to see what she'd done. She was going crazy, every other thought running out of control. In a panic, she reached for the soap and began to scrub away the pheromone-laced slick before the whole apartment reeked of Omega arousal.

She was in the kitchen when Corday returned. Looking up from the simple pasta she'd prepared for dinner, Claire offered a smile. "Welcome back."

Good and sweaty, Corday's cockeyed smile was quickly hidden when he pulled the pungent sweater over his head. "Just let me grab a quick shower. We'll eat, then we'll go."

Nodding, smiling in gratitude for his effort, she announced, "Dinner will be ready when you're done."

Once Corday had disappeared behind the bathroom door, she retrieved the little white pill that had been hidden away days ago. Crushing it to a fine powder, she mixed the drug into his serving.

Claire knew no amount of soap could wash away the pheromones lingering in the bathroom. When he took longer than usual, red up to her ears, she tried to ignore Corday's muffled grunt, ashamed she'd put him in such a position.

Another stifled noise, an extended curse, and the sound of the water ended.

By the time Corday emerged, her embarrassment had faded back into familiar fatigue, and she offered the dish.

Between the run, jacking off in the shower, and the sleeping pill she'd hidden in his food, Corday was out cold in less than an hour. Claire dressed in the sweaty clothes he'd prepared for her, threw a blanket over the Beta who'd been so kind, and left to find her Omegas.

***

The harsher chill of the Lower Reaches was underscored by light flurries dampening Claire's clothes. The distance was far, her pace dangerous for an exhausted woman about ready to drop.

It seemed they had been anticipating her, a small group of Omegas already at the cracked entrance, candle in hand. Doubled over once safely inside, Claire struggled to catch her breath, croaking, "Senator Kantor has a plan. He can provide food and real heat-suppressants."

"How?" It was Lilian, the redhead, who brought the candle closer.

"That is what we must discuss. He wishes to break us up into smaller cells, smuggle us to safe houses where armed Enforcers could stand guard. Or, should we demand it, they will bring rations here."

"The Enforcers are hunted down in the streets." Deriding, Lilian snorted, "They'll all be dead in less than a year. Who would bring the food then, Claire?"

Too tired to be patient, Claire stood up straight. "I'm only offering options. The group must decide for itself if they want instant slavery or difficult freedom."

It was then Claire realized no more Omegas had come to join them. Nona was nowhere to be seen. The only faces around that candle were Lilian and two very unfriendly looking women.

"We have already decided," Lilian snarled, swinging a rock in her fist.

The world spun, sharp pain erupting beside Claire's ear. Broken pavement and scattered refuse scraped her legs, her listless body pulled deeper into their shelter. Trying to focus past the ringing in her skull, her unsteady eyes searched for Nona in the crowd, only to find the older woman restrained, struggling to get free.

She called out to her, begged the Omegas not to give in to fear, and felt a hand fist her hair to wrench her away. Dragged to a storage cell, Claire was shoved inside, the sound of something heavy heaved to bar her only exit.

Disoriented, surrounded by the dark, her green eyes stared blankly at cracked walls.

They were grey.

Her broken laugh echoed back at her. Tasting blood in her mouth, she turned so the icy ground might cool the throbbing lump growing on her skull.

But there was no time to rest. She had to get up.

It took great effort to uncurl from a ball and crawl to the door. Standing hunched, Claire screamed out her story, told them not to lose themselves in desperation and panic, to think rationally and see that Shepherd would never pay a bounty, that the whole thing had been a trap just to snare her. To stop before they all made themselves slaves.

She could not budge the rubble blocking her in. She could not scream loud enough.

Claire only had so much voice, and as it left her, so did her ability to differentiate fantasy from reality.

As she slid down the wall, the dream began.

So much running, the wave of madness at her back, but Shepherd was there holding back the dark, his arm upraised. She ran straight for him, close enough to smell him before her feet skidded to a halt. There were screams, furious screams of the Omegas at her back. The wave of noise was getting closer. Terrified eyes went back to Shepherd, back to the man standing like a stone in the chaos as he crooked his finger.

She took another step.

The dream began again.

Light came on in her cell, the single dangling fixture above her flickering in its sorry state. The hum of the old bulb and the filament inside drew her to her scraped knees and then wobbling feet.

The mob. She could hear them, their shouts closing in. Any moment they would come for her. She would run, because she always ran. And she would find him, because he was always there, waiting.

Again and again.

Her head turned towards the door, where it seemed inevitable his large form would fill the portal, that she would see the same roughened armor, the same Da'rin markings crawling up his neck... those eyes.

The intensity with which Shepherd stared seemed unnatural.

Whatever he saw in her expression made the giant crouch down, as if to make himself seem smaller. The Alpha reached out a hand, slowly, so as not to frighten.

He'd never crouched in the dream before.

Claire closed her eyes, certain she had finally lost her mind, then that sound came... that long pined for purr, loud and confident, reassuring her that all was well.

"Come to me, little one." Even his rough voice seemed perfect, melodic as the words passed scarred lips. Coaxing, non-threatening, he added, "You will not be punished."

The thread was pulsating, whispering to her as it did, tempting her to step forward and take her Alpha's hand. That he was calling her. That he missed her.

Claire had no idea what made her say the words, but they came softly, like a confession. "You've been haunting my sleep. Every time I close my eyes, you're there."

"You've been in my dreams, as well." Shepherd crooned so deep she imagined she could feel the vibration change her on a cellular level. "You've been singing to me, little one."

Dazed, she pulled in a breath, smelling the scent that was supposed to be with her—the familiar musk of that Alpha. "What did I sing?"

A smile was in his eyes, the skin at the corners crinkling. His fingers flicked, beckoning her, and Claire found herself mesmerized by the movement. "Come."

In the distance, there were sounds, frightening things of the mob from her dreams. Soon she would have to run... or she could choose to end it.

It took three weak steps before she was standing directly before him. Looking at the male who, even crouched, was at her eye-level, Claire did not take his hand. Instead she sagged against him, demanding in an exhausted voice, "Purr."

He did, turning to study the disoriented woman resting her head on his shoulder, weighing the beauty of her extended groan broadcasting that there was nothing else in the world that had ever been so soothing as the noise rumbling from his chest.

Massive arms wrapped around her the instant she began slipping to the floor.

Shepherd stood.

Claire didn't see the blue-eyed soldier take up position as guard. She didn't know Shepherd took off his coat, or feel her body being stripped of clothing that reeked of another male.

She was laid in the heat of his coat, wrapped in the scent of the Alpha. Unfocused and uncaring, she felt his body settle between her thighs, Shepherd a furnace compared to the cold room.

"You are lost, little one. I will bring you home."

She mumbled a reply, her vague mind in agreement. Warm hands, callused and reassuring, ran down her stomach, spreading her legs wide. Before she could complain, the firm press of lips and the flicking dart of a tongue ran over the part of her no one had ever touched in such a way.

Shepherd tasted her, ensuring she'd remained untainted by another... purely his.

Finding her uncorrupted, the Alpha growled savagely. At the sound, her body bowed, her pussy responding with a stream of slick. Shepherd noisily sucked it all into his mouth, swallowing, lapping madly.

There was nothing gentle in the way he scoured her clean.

A choked cry and Claire's eyes flew open. All she could see in the haze was his face buried between her thighs, his eyes closed as if the feast were perfection. He sensed her attention, gun-metal gaze flashing. The lower part of his face hidden, Shepherd continued to devour her even as he growled, "You have been exceptionally disobedient. A difficult and defiant mate."

Panting, crying out when he flicked her clit, Claire argued with the apparition, "It's your own damn fault! You're a tyrant. You expect things I don't understand. I hardly know a thing about you. You don't listen... keep me locked underground. How would you like to live in prison?"

Shepherd chuckled evilly, gripped her hips to still her writhing, and gluttonously pulled her dripping cunt closer.

Fighting gasps and throaty moans, she accused, "All you ever do is fuck me!"

She felt his teeth skim her folds, his lips curling into a smile. Shepherd's answer was rich, licentious. "I greatly enjoy fucking you."

She wished he'd disappear and the dream could end, but not until she fought her broken voice to accuse, "You force me."

He rebutted, his teeth lightly biting the little nub his thumb exposed from its hood, causing her to twitch frantically so he might prove his point. "I always ensure you feel pleasure when we mate."

Breathing out an unhappy moan, she whined, "That is not true."

"I punished you once by rutting you without your gratification, and ascertained it was not the best way to discipline your bad behavior. I have not done it since." Once the words were finished, he attacked her with rapid flicks of his tongue, a pleased growl coming from his smiling lips when his little one began practically sobbing from the attention her trapped hips could not escape.

When Claire was right at the cusp of falling further into delirium, Shepherd licked a trail up her body, leaving her aching pussy neglected so he might pin her down. A nipple was captured, suckled almost too hard until the bud lengthened. Distantly, she heard the grate of a zipper and then sucked in the heady smell of potent Alpha musk once his member was exposed. The bulbous head butted against her, and ever so slowly he eased into a place that was fragile and tight from neglect.

With her distracted, Shepherd tried to take the one thing he had not been able to coax from her yet. He captured her parted, moaning lips to tempt out a kiss. It woke her from the spell, her black lashes flew open.

It was not a dream.

All she could see were the lust-filled silver eyes, challenging her to participate even as Shepherd dipped his tongue into her mouth. He invaded—so she might sample how perfect she tasted—and began to thrust.

She tried to take her mouth away. To prevent it, he cupped her cheek, running his lips over hers as much as he desired, knowing she recognized what he'd done, how he'd defied her last barrier, and fought for the kiss she continued to deny him.

The feel of his cock—it was all so intoxicating, consuming, and infinitely disturbing. Claire grew frenzied once he began pounding with vigor. Borderline violent, Shepherd fucked in earnest until she was writhing and crying out, needing release, needing sleep, needing him to give her all those things and more. Turning her head to the side, his palm braced her cheek so that his lips could suck a trail down the exposed side of her throat.

The feeling of his mouth, the rasp of warm tongue on cold flesh, and frustration blended with delusional ecstasy. The second her pussy clenched and her undoing began, he shoved in deep, his knot swelling huge, stretching her mercilessly. Claire's orgasm raged so hard it hurt, her pussy milking him desperately as Shepherd bared his teeth and bit down brutally atop the scar on her shoulder—the scar that made her his. A crunch sounded, teeth broke skin, and blood began to flow.

Claire's throat could only offer a silent scream, her agony ignored as he ferociously tightened his jaw. With her trapped by his massive knot, there was no escape, made worse when her pussy spasmed and blended pleasure into the pain with each spurt of hot come the Alpha dumped inside her.

The Omega was sobbing when it was finished, bleeding badly, and so overcome that she no longer knew where she was.

"Shhh," he whispered, licking at the running blood, hushing her gently while she wept. He gave her the purr she'd wanted, petting and stroking, his lips at her ear. "Now you may sleep, little one."

Everything had been too much. Too much fear, too much heartache, too much anger, too much desire. Overwhelmed, Claire closed her eyes and gave over to the thing her body needed most. Shepherd tucked her limp arms into the sleeves of his coat. Hitching her about his waist, his knot still joining them, he walked out the door, her naked body and their joining covered by the drape of worn leather.

Outside the waste facility, the Omegas were being herded onto transport prepared to take them to the Undercroft, a few snarling, others screaming, but the majority simply scarfing down supplement bars his Followers were passing out.

Claire missed it all in her dead slumber.

Chapter 7

Claire felt no warm haze, no fulfilling sense of contentment upon waking. Instead, a deep-seated ache drew her brows tight, only growing worse when she shifted. Someone had run her over with a transport rig, wrung her out... left her wasted. Confused, her lashes parted, and Claire saw nothing but subterranean gloom and walls of concrete.

It was the smell that brought it all together, the nest of familiar, soft blankets rich with the scent of her mate.

Not mate... Claire had to remind herself. Shepherd.

She hated that his stink offered reassurance in her discomfort, that the thread was humming delightedly, telling her it was okay to feel weak so long as he was nearby to watch over her... that everything was back as it should be. The worm pulsed and grew warm in her chest. It was that manipulative pair-bond which had distorted her in the first place—Shepherd's influence, which had broken her apart day after day when she ignored her mate's call to return—that led to exhaustion and hallucinations. Now it was writhing in contentment, spinning a web of the seductive lie of shelter and safety.

It seemed stronger than before, that cord humming between them felt tighter in her chest. Was it because of his total victory over her? Or maybe because she had stumbled straight to him in her craving for sleep? Claire didn't know. All she knew was that her struggles, her denial and stubbornness, had been for nothing.

They were bound. Even in her hiding, he'd exercised control.

That grey-walled room was not shelter. It was her prison. Shepherd had her in his cage, she was back under his thumb... and she would probably never leave that room again.

Swallowing down distress, Claire recognized his great weight dipping the mattress at her side, her thigh flush to his back as if she'd pressed near while she slept. Shepherd was facing the wall, his elbows on his knees, staring forward, lost in thought.

Licking dry lips, Claire thought to scoot away, only to fall back to the pillows with a curse. The pain was great, shooting from her shoulder so sharply it was all she could do to breathe.

The broad expanse of bare muscled back rippled, Shepherd turning his head to look at the recaptured woman. His silver eyes were blank, the Alpha's air not one of impending punishment, nor was it one of offered comfort. He seemed static, yet those mercurial eyes were watching her as if she were troublesome and easy to crush.

Abashed by such an expression, Claire glanced away, her attention turning to the blood-soaked gauze at her shoulder. Unsure why she felt guilty under his appraisal, why she was tempted to apologize, she focused on the task of peeking under the bandage. What she found almost made her retch. The wound may have been cleaned and dressed at some point while she slept, but it was an oozing, sluggishly bleeding mess, swollen and bruised and utterly disgusting.

No wonder it hurt so badly. Shepherd had maimed her.

He reached out a hand, pulling back the gauze to see the bite mark for himself. He seemed pleased. "That will scar nicely."

It would scar horribly... twenty times worse than the last mark he'd made.

Unforgiving silver eyes bore down on the woman, watching as she pressed back the dressing and tried to calm her breath. "Perhaps now you will remember that you have a mate," he said.

Tired of intimidation and fear and silence, she forced her body to sit up. Ignoring the agony of an unresponsive arm, her green eyes flared, her small hand covering the dressing as if to shield it from him. Appalled, she growled, "You will not be punished? Then what is this? How would you like it if I tore a chunk out of you?"

Shepherd raised a brow and challenged, "I am your mate. You may mark me if you wish."

Something in his words caused a jolting craving to chomp so strong her lips peeled back from her teeth. With a snap of speed, Claire rolled out from under the blankets, her nails already digging little red moons into Shepherd's biceps as she scrambled to the position so she might sink in her teeth at the juncture of shoulder and neck.

Somewhere in the haze of action, she recognized the beast was holding still, that no great swiping arm had sent her flying in response to her aggression. Her instinctive reaction had been so very quick, so mindless, that she only caught herself a second before punching her mark into the proper patch of skin.

An unexpected wave of dizziness made her vision swim, overwhelming nausea snapping her out of madness.

After a shaky breath, reason returned.

Confused by how badly she still wished to bite, how everything inside her told her it was her right—that she needed it—Claire slumped, exhausted. Shepherd's hands were already on her waist, steadying her as she dropped her forehead to his shoulder.

Flesh to flesh, he smelled like he was hers, the thread gratified by his proximity.

Why did it have to feel so good when he pulled her closer, holding her so that she might find her strength?

After a minute, she clumsily unhooked her claws from his arm, back in control of her urges, stubborn and resolute to resist. But her head was still spinning when she glanced up. Liquid mercury watched as he always watched her, like a wolf licking his chops. She made a move to climb off his lap and return to the warmth of the bed, but his arms held her firm, settling her body where she straddled his thighs.

A finger traced down her spine, a reminder she was naked... a state he had seen her in so many times there was little shame in it.

"There are topics that must be discussed." It was said conversationally, but his expression was daring argument. "To begin, you will tell me where you have been for the last eight days."

Her voice seemed to catch, worn from screaming at her sister Omegas so this very scenario might be prevented. "I was offered shelter after I collapsed in the street, by a man who was kind to me, who listened, and who tried to help."

The heat of his massive palms kneaded deeply into her lower back, pressing her closer. "Who was this man?"

Claire shook her head, frowning and bracing herself to receive punishment for the words she was about to speak. "I won't let you kill him because he was noble."

There was the slightest of squints above a warning smirk. Shepherd's voice crooned, oddly complacent, and a total lie. "Perhaps I wish to reward the Beta whose stench saturated your clothing. After all, he tended to my runaway, foolish mate."

"No. You wish to know how to reach Senator Kantor so you might string him up from the Citadel." Claire knew the Omegas he'd captured would spill every word she had told them in their fear. They might have lost themselves in despair and starvation, but Claire had been made stronger by being fed as Shepherd's pet, and she would not give the Alpha information to help hunt down anyone who might resist his occupation.

Threading large fingers into her hair, Shepherd began to comb out the tangles. "Do you know where he is?"

"I do not. He came to me. But even if I had learned his location, I would not tell you."

"Do you think that your loyalty to those men will save them?"

She straightened her spine and fought to keep sadness from weakening her voice. "They were the only ones who offered to actually help, who wanted nothing in return, respected me as a person—not an object... I will not say a word that might help you hurt them." After a sniff, she raised her chin, all defiance and haughty determination. "You may have the Omegas under your control, you may have me back in this room, but you will never claim my integrity or honor."

A finger traced the line of her jaw, his silver eyes almost soft as they searched her face. "You are still so defiant."

"I am still Claire."

Unexpectedly, the purr rumbled, soaking into her, soothing her rankled belligerence. When Shepherd spoke, it was indulgent. "You are... wayward and foolishly noble... I find it is not disappointing."

Why was he looking at her gently? Why was he saying nice things? Narrowing her eyes, suspicious even as the purr made it all better, Claire tensed.

Shepherd's thumb brushed her lips. "Did you miss me, little one?"

113

The dark fan of her lashes lowered, Claire was unwilling to answer. She had missed him. Missed his smell and the purr, missed the calm he cultivated with precision. But her desire for such things was only the result of the bond. She had not missed the constant feeling of being trapped—watching day by day as more pieces of herself were peeled away.

"Answer me, little one." He used that power he had, making the thread knock about in her chest.

Looking lost, her emerald eyes met his. "You have invaded my mind."

"And your body," he added, holding her a little firmer.

"And my body," Claire agreed, her expression brokenly resigned. "Is that what you want to hear?"

Pinching her chin so she could not look away, he warned, "You will not run again."

The pair-bond had grown so overwhelming that even if she did, there was no chance for true freedom. The dreams, the waking hallucinations, Shepherd would be with her no matter where she tried to hide. But knowing that and accepting it were not the same thing. Claire wanted freedom, she wanted to choose.

"Shepherd," she spoke his name, a thing that was rare unless in the throes of passion. "I needed to breathe fresh air. I needed to see the sky."

His purring ceased.

"The sky," Shepherd spat the word as if the idea were overrated. A deep breath rattled in his chest. "You think you know what prison is, little one. You do not. In prison, one is surrounded by the worst possible breed of men. If I wanted food or water, I had to kill for it. Shelter, supplies... everything was hard-earned. What you call rape is nothing compared to what the dregs indulge in. You live in safety and comfort. I tend to you and soothe—see to your needs." His voice grew utterly disgusted. "And still you pine for your sky."

Shepherd had never once shared personal opinion. Intrigued at the strangeness of such a statement, Claire's brows furrowed and she said, "I can't decipher which of your Da'rin markings explains what crime put you in the Undercroft."

Ignoring her hinted question, Shepherd smirked. "That term you use for it—the Undercroft— I find it amusing. A poetic word used to describe a place of darkness, filled with the pleas of thousands scraping at the doors to get out. And as for crimes... crime is irrelevant. I was never condemned to your Undercroft. I was born there."

Shepherd was a man who remorselessly created suffering—one who understood the dark workings of the human mind as if they were second nature—but such a monstrous history could not be true. Claire stared, looking for the flaw, for the lie.

Tight words betrayed his irritation. "You claimed to know nothing of me. Now I have spoken, and you are mute."

She inched her face a little closer, a line growing between her brows. "Females are not sentenced to the Undercroft. They labor on the farm levels, segregated from men until rehabilitated. What you claim cannot be true. Such an act is against our laws."

Shepherd laughed dryly. "Your laws? What do you know of the cage you live in and the false histories you've been trained to recite?"

Cheeks flaming from his mockery, Claire shrank back. "So in isolating me from the world, your goal is to make me deranged like you?"

The question seemed to momentarily confuse him. After a brief pause, he answered, "I want you to become amenable, to stop resisting, and to look objectively instead of with bruised emotions that will never serve you."

"And I am just supposed to forget what you've done?" Hurt sat in her eyes, Claire listing his sins. "You took me against my will, offered no help to my cause... only seized for your own. You have captured the Omegas and even now hold them captive so you might give them away to strangers. You see us as objects. How can you not understand why I feel so resistant, why I am afraid?"

He purred, almost inaudibly, once she claimed to feel fear. So intent on her expression, so very concentrated in his regard, his hand cupped her cheek. Large thumb stroking soft skin, he explained, "Your own kind betrayed you. Do not waste your thoughts on those who are unworthy."

She could feel her eyes well, knew he would not let her look away, and forced herself to ask, "Were any of them hurt?"

"No wounds of consequence. Three will be hanged."

Horrified, Claire whispered, "For what reason?"

Shepherd hardened his expression, flexing the arm that chained her to his lap. "They attacked my mate and tried to sell you to me... thought to barter a life I already own to ensure their comfort. Do not imagine they had any regard for the others either. Those women had no intention of returning to share the spoils."

Claire clutched at the hand he held to her face, pleading. "Please don't kill them. Lilian and the others were starving, afraid, and desperate."

"So were you"—his narrowed eyes flared—"more afraid than they were. And you were, and are still, trying to be their champion."

Looking down, full of sadness, Claire muttered, "I am a piss-poor champion."

"You did fairly well considering the odds," he acknowledged quietly. "Your flaw was assuming there is good in Thólos, when there is not. That is why you lost."

"I know you're wrong. Some of those women are my friends. They are good people. Those who attacked me... I don't know them well, but I would rather show mercy than condemn desperate, starving women tempted by the lie of food you broadcasted on your leaflet."

"And that is why you are weak"—it seemed almost a compliment—"and why I am strong."

"You are stronger than me," Claire acknowledged, studying the Da'rin markings on Shepherd's shoulder, unsure how many dead were represented in that patch of skin. "You're faster, have power, but you lack something great. And you will never find it in the life you live."

"Do I?" It was as if he knew what she was going to say, found her opinion juvenile and cute. "Do you speak of love?"

She shook her head, black tangled hair waving around her shoulders. "Not love. Anyone can love."

"Then what, little sage?"

"Humanity... the source of joy. You may have had it once, but whatever life you've lived has eaten it away."

He hummed at her, unconcerned with her judgment. "I understand humanity at its basest level, and have far more experience in the world than you do, little one. The way the citizens are behaving— such as those women I am going to hang no matter how much you may beg or cry—proves the point that they were never good, even before starvation. Suffering merely draws out the true nature of each life festering under the Dome."

"The way you speak, you make it sound as if you believe you are offering enlightenment by knowingly crafting misery," Claire scoffed, shaking her head, surprised he had not just started fucking her to shut her mouth.

It was the same stormy fury that rolled through his eyes when her words displeased him.

118

Claire was still afraid—afraid of the monster who could so easily crush her, afraid of the effects of the bond—but Shepherd seemed tranquil and almost willing to let her speak.

"The books you keep," she breathed softly, looking to the shelving across the room. "You have such a strange collection... a veritable training manual on how to be a dictator. But then there are soft things: poetry, writings by great spiritual leaders and virtuous human beings. Do you read them to try to seek what you are missing?"

He stated with pride, "I am The Shepherd. I lead the flock."

She whispered the words, mesmerized by the exchange, "Through terrorism?"

"Your naiveté is like that of a child. Under this Dome, injustice runs rampant. Thólos is a cesspool filled with corruption, greed, apathy, and vice—a breeding ground of lies. Weakness must be purged, deceptions exposed, and punishment suffered."

Her thickly lashed green eyes went wide. "This is some kind of trial?"

"You have grown wiser, Miss O'Donnell."

The fact he had used her surname was chilling. Her end of the thread began to hum out of tune, the connection to such a creature unwanted and abhorrent. "You don't want power at all... you want the city to wallow in what your breach has inspired. You want to watch us squirm."

A conceited smirk, an evil thing, distorted scarred lips. "Continue, little one."

Slight understanding of the man and his reasoning came together. "You think you are some kind of champion... like Premier Callas, or—"

Snapping in anger, Shepherd cut her off, "Your precious Premier is no more. I ripped him apart with my bare hands, and caution you against speaking his name in my presence."

To be Premier was to be the ultimate servant of Thólos: a hereditary position held by the family that had erected the Dome, and served until death. They were immaculate, lived wisely, and led by example. Yet Shepherd's hate was personal... unexplainable. Claire had to know. Heart racing, she tempted fate, and whispered, "Why?"

"Your Enforcers are dead, your Premier rots in pieces, and soon every Senator will swing outside the Citadel so that all Thólos might breathe the true stink of their corruption." Shepherd placed his lips to her neck and pulled in her scent, flexing his hips to press his growing erection between the soft legs wrapped around him. "So you see, there is no one to save you. You have only me."

At those words, panic surged, her mind racing past the point of dread. If Shepherd hadn't started purring at that very instant, she might have begun to scream.

Large hands went to his belt. He felt her tremble and resist as he withdrew his member, restraining his weakened mate on his lap easily. Feeling the feminine curves nurtured by the food he'd provided, he gave a hungry growl. The instant she was remotely wet enough, he lowered her down on his straining erection.

The pace was almost languid. Her head buried against his shoulder as he lifted and lowered her, Claire's panic broken apart by distracting debauchery.

There would be no escape, all her fighting had been for nothing—these things he whispered in her ear.

She would not show her face, or her silent tears—her only view the sight of his thick cock, shiny with slick, infiltrating her body, just as his taunts penetrated her mind.

Shepherd stroked a hand up to grip her neck, pulled her closer until her breasts were flush to his chest, the location of their bond in contact. He held her so wet, green eyes were compelled to meet his. "Kiss me."

Claire felt it begin all over again. "No."

It was his show. It was always his show. Her life was his, her body too. But her lips were her own.

Her defiance only excited Shepherd more. With a low, animal growl, what had been unhurried became an all-out carnal attack. He turned them about, bouncing her on the mattress to pound the scented, pretty hole that sheathed him so perfectly. She screamed, filled the air with sobbed moans of his name. Shepherd held her by the nape, felt the strength of her climax lock on to his cock as he swelled and secured her to him. And though his hips were trapped by the knot, it did not stop the pad of his thumb from grinding against Claire's swollen clit.

He was merciless, pushed her past pleasure and to a point of overburdened sensation.

She tried to writhe away from his finger, the friction too strong, but could do nothing, pinned as she was. Begging in breathless catches of sound, Claire panted, "Shepherd, please stop."

Watching her lips form the words, dissecting the tortured desire and uncontrolled pleasure, he rubbed even faster. Snarling like a beast, still painting her womb with spurts of cream, he demanded, "Who do you belong to?"

There were tears leaking from eyes squeezed shut as she jerked and twitched from his abuse of her clit and the cramping orgasm, prolonged too far. "Pleeease, please stop... I can't..."

"WHO DO YOU BELONG TO?"

She was going to die; it was too much, the sensation so great it was agony. Everything went white, as if the world was made of nothing but blinding, horrid light that stripped her bare. Back arching, she sucked in air, like the first gasping breath of a newborn, and felt another wave of devastating contractions in her core. With a face full of pained pleasure, Claire gasped, "I belong to you!"

"That's right, little one," came a voice as if leagues away. The pinch on her nerves abated and she sobbed when the over-strong, extended climax began to abate. More waves of hot semen burned her from the inside when Shepherd purred, "You belong only to me."

The punishment had been brutal, and it took him almost an hour to soothe her trembling muscles and ragged breath. Eyes shut tight, Claire burrowed into him, pressing hard, worried that should the contact vanish, she might cease to exist.

With a stroke down her hip and back up again, the monster explained in a low, soft rumble. "If I ever smell another man's scent saturating you again, I will hunt down the male and rip off his limbs while you watch... then I will fuck you in the pool of his blood."

Her fingers simply clawed where she clung, digging in deep. "When you speak that way, it frightens me."

Strangely, he hushed her as if comforting a child, gathering her tighter in his embrace.

Chapter 8

He just couldn't believe it. Shaking his head, hurting for her, Corday fought boiling anger. Rumors had spread like wildfire, varying stories of how an enclave of Omegas had been rescued.

That was the term Dome Broadcast used to describe it. Rescued.

And Claire was gone. Deep in his gut, Corday felt responsible—that he should have known the Omega would do what she felt was best—and hated himself for not seeing the signs.

Waking up on that lumpy couch, a crick in his neck from the odd angle, he'd realized at once what she'd done. Leaping to his feet, cursing up a storm, Corday had run out the door.

There had been no need to search, his hours racing through the city wasted. Had he simply turned on his COMscreen, a distorted version of the story— including footage of emaciated women accepting food—would have played on repeat. There had been no shot of Claire, or even Shepherd for that matter. But a short Beta known to be Shepherd's second-in-command was featured, offering blankets to the Omegas and directing Followers to see them to safety.

A lie.

Corday didn't know how Shepherd had found them, but after seeing the flyer and the outrageous bounty, he suspected that one of Claire's friends had betrayed her.

The thought broke his heart.

The Enforcer knew Thólos, understood what she was up against. Innocent Claire was too idealistic, too sweet, and no matter how willful she was, still Omega. She saw the world through the eyes of a caretaker, a nurturer—not a warrior.

From the look of the icy grounds surrounding the capture, from the steam of starving women's exhaled breath, it was the freezing Lower Reaches that had sheltered Claire's group—a dangerous place where more than just the subzero weather could kill you.

Corday had made his way into the mist to see for himself, disguised as a looter to pick through the warren, blending in with the rest of the vultures already poaching the meager goods left behind.

Claire's smell lingered in the air, heady with anxiety, powerful from the sweat she must have worked up when she ran to her friends. Corday followed it, ignoring the deserted personal items scattered around the rooms, the garbage. The trail ended at a closet, where—once the door was pushed open—he found trapped air that reeked of sex. Shepherd had fucked her the moment he'd found her. That was clear not only from the smell, but the sight of the discarded sweater and pants Claire had been wearing. His clothes—the ones Corday had specially prepared for her earlier that day.

Crouching down, he lifted the fabric and brought it to his nose, pulling in a breath of the Omega, bowing his head, feeling like a failure.

It could not end this way.

He may have failed Claire, but her information about the pills had brought to light other Omegas in need, and the Enforcers—led by Brigadier Dane—were already preparing to strike. Corday would help them like he'd promised. After all, what was the point of resistance if one didn't actually fight back?

***

Corday had a difficult time finding respect for a woman like Brigadier Dane. Dane's arrogance and short-sighted need to constantly remind him about his father's crimes and subsequent incarceration had set them at odds from the first moment he'd met his commanding officer. But something had changed in Dane during the months since the city fell. It was clear that the Alpha female harbored the massive weight of survivor's guilt. Dane tried much harder, spoke much less, and seemed as grimly determined as Corday to right at least one wrong if she could.

The weather was nasty. Even at midday, it was almost dark, the swollen sky over-dome just as unwelcoming as the guards outside the chem pusher's den. When Corday arrived to join Dane's tactical assault, he could smell drugs cooking, the bitter, chemical tinge tainting the air. More so, he could hear the drugged, needy calls of the women, begging for release from wherever the saggy faced dealer had them locked away.

There were about twelve men on the premises. Half were armed with Enforcer-grade artillery they should not have had access to. Guns slung over their shoulders, faces devoid of emotion, the thugs were habituated to the vileness surrounding them. From Dane's intel, the Enforcers now knew which sleaze ran the show; an older, stocky Alpha named Otto. The Brigadier's orders were to keep him alive for questioning.

They needed to know who had supplied those men with those guns. Were they affiliated with Shepherd's Followers? Were there other cartels with artillery that could be confiscated?

Customers were already shuffling in with offerings to trade, twitching with the need to knot a heated Omega. It seemed something as simple as a fresh piece of fruit or a bag of rice could get an Alpha or Beta laid. There were stockpiles of food, crates stacked in a guarded corner that could be put to better use once impounded.

Taking down these men might potentially fund the beginnings of a true rebellion.

Led by Brigadier Dane, with Corday at her back, the team of twelve armored Enforcers breached the concrete compound in tactical formation. All targets were eliminated without question, the infiltration choreographed to a precision even Shepherd would have admired.

While Dane took down the men bent over tables cooking drugs, Corday's team turned a corner and passed into the back of the building. Nearing where the Omegas were corralled, the Enforcers, like all humans, found themselves susceptible to the lust-inducing pheromones mixed with the stink of human filth. The animal inside Corday sniffed, instantaneously enticed, while the human who controlled such urges found all he saw repulsive. The view was sickening. Six women were chained to the wall, collars around their necks like dogs. Two were so emaciated from the continuous estrous, Corday was not sure how they were still breathing.

Each captive was equidistant—just a bit too far from the others to touch. A few were still being rutted by Alphas; oblivious to the soldiers bearing down upon them. There was no mercy with the city a war zone. A single shot to the head and the offenders died, too caught up in the knot to disengage. In the end, only three of the savages—including the necessary Otto—had been taken alive and bound in the middle of the room. The Enforcers began unchaining Omegas, preparing to move them as soon as possible before one of the officers instinctively fell into a rut from the pheromones.

There were things Corday had seen in his short years as an Enforcer, crimes so vulgar he just could not believe anyone was capable of committing them. It turned out that the horrors in that Omega kennel were only the beginning. Behind a chained meat locker lay the spent bodies of numerous skeletal creatures. The emaciated corpses of eleven murdered Omegas, bruised, beaten, gazing out of lifeless eyes at the nothing they had become were haphazardly piled up, frozen from the cold that kept them from rotting.

Brigadier Dane stared, the Alpha female slack-jawed, seeing one little girl who looked so much like her missing sister, it took her a moment to register the shouting of her men. Tearing her eyes away, she rushed toward the outcry. One of the Omegas, a female freshly caught and still free of the drug's full effect, held a shard of glass that dripped with blood. Naked, she stood over Otto and his thugs, sawing through the bound gangster's neck until her hand bled.

She'd killed their source of information.

Corday was talking to the Omega in hushed tones, trying to soothe her, to get her to drop the glass, but nothing seemed to get through her zombie-like expression. "Shh-shh, it's all right, put down the glass. We're Enforcers, and we're going to get you someplace safe, ma'am."

Looking to the youth holding out his hands as if to placate her, her broken voice managed, "They killed my Doug, my baby."

"Please, put down the glass."

Glazed eyes rolled back to the dead men who had chained her up, who had taken her life. There was not even a moment of hesitation. She jammed the bloody weapon so deep into her throat, the gush of blood was immediate.

Corday rushed forward, putting his hands to her neck.

Brigadier Dane knew there was no way to save the female from the gaping slash she'd sliced into her own throat, no matter how hard the frantic Beta tried. But there had been ways to save all the females piled up in that meat locker—had the Enforcers taken notice, had they acted months ago. Instead, they had been too busy mustering, plotting, and doing nothing.

In the hearts of all who watched, all feelings of victory faded, dripped away as that Omega's blood stained the floor. Dane crouched down and closed the dead Omega's eyes as she spoke their prayer.

When the incantation to the Mother Goddess of Omegas was complete, Dane's voice hardened. Orders were barked. The tower of food was disassembled and loaded onto transport. The heat-addled Omegas were carted away.

The bodies had to be left behind. There was nothing that could be done for the dead.

All the drugs were dumped, spilling together, filling the air with noxious fumes—the perfect recipe for the absolution of fire. Corday struck the flame, destroying the counterfeit heat-suppressants, the methamphetamines... the evidence of atrocities and the Enforcers' part in purifying it. But the shell of the building still stood.

Thólos was fireproof.

***

Tired, Claire stretched her legs out from under warm blankets and pressed her feet to the ground. She felt… off, saturated with the lethargy that comes before illness, and was grateful Shepherd was not in the room to paw at her as he always did when she woke. He had punished her for her resistance, had frightened, then placated, back to his old tricks of trying to warp her mind.

Sitting on the edge of the bed, she rubbed the sleep from her eyes and frowned at the ache in her shoulder. In the room, everything was where it had been the last time she had been locked inside. Except her painting of poppies. It was skewed, the paper less crisp, as if having been handled repeatedly. Denying her impulse to center it, Claire studied the flowers, certain Shepherd had done the same in her absence.

Considering the great rage which had blared from his side of the link at the onset of her escape, there was no sign of such wrath about the cell. No furniture was broken. Her meager things were exactly where she had left them, almost as if she had never been gone. Even the bed sheets were the same; stale, unchanged in her absence.

Moving at a snail's pace towards the bathroom, Claire peeled off the gauze on her shoulder and stood under warm water. It was hard to move her arm without pain, shampoo stung her wound, and she found herself gritting her teeth at the discomfort it caused her simply to become clean.

As if he had known she would want to bathe upon waking, there was a sterile gauze pad and tape waiting on the counter. Wanting to cover the ugly

131

mark so her churning stomach would stop threatening to spill each time she looked at it, Claire dressed the bite. While pressing down the tape, mindful of the bruising, her eyes caught something that shouldn't be. The small bin they used for their laundry displayed one of her dresses peeking out near the top. Considering she had been gone for eight days, it struck her as strange. Pulling it out, her brows shot up. The fabric smelled of her, but it reeked of Shepherd's semen... as if he had been sniffing it as he masturbated before coming on her clothes.

The idea brought an unwelcome twinge between her legs, and Claire unthinkingly dug deeper, only to find almost every item of her clothing had been treated the same way. Why would he do that— or, more importantly, why did it smell so good? Realizing she still had the first dress pressed to her nose, a wave of embarrassment made her cheeks burn. Claire quickly stuffed the offensive laundry back down.

Cool water was splashed on her face and the fever seemed to pass.

There was something about the act he'd committed. In all her days of freedom, she had fought not to think of Shepherd, not to question how their separation might have affected him. Claire had not allowed herself to wonder if he had suffered as she had. Her denial of his call, her denial of the bond, it had twisted her. What had it done to him? Had he worried she might have been hurt? Even the bounty had stipulated she must be brought in undamaged to claim the reward. The man had placed a great deal of confidence in the greed of others... and it looked like his assessment had been correct.

Claire left the bathroom, left her flushed reflection, and began to pace.

Absently, she looked about and found her earlier assessment was incorrect. The room was just not right. It began with the bedding, it was unsatisfactory. It had to be replaced. She stripped it off, feeling slightly better when fresh linen was laid out. Her painting had to be moved, to be centered. A headache began to pound, the lump on her skull throbbing. She began to pace some more. One moment she was hot, the next cold. Yet no matter if she sweated or shivered, she was thoroughly uncomfortable.

Worry for the Omegas agitated the forefront of her thoughts. Shepherd had assured her no one had been wounded. But what of Lilian? What of her cohorts? Had he murdered them? Was he stringing them up that very second?

Claire's stomach rolled, and for a moment she felt truly ill. The feeling passed, swamping her with dread and leaving her empty. This was it. Green eyes appraised drab, grey walls, sweeping the room. This was her life—a life tethered to a man obsessed with keeping her hidden away; who was going to hang three women because they had tried to collect the bounty he'd offered. A possessive monster who wielded evil as a tool... a fiend who would say terrifying things and then cuddle her back to a sense of false comfort.

Shepherd was admittedly evil. They were incompatible—in needs, in ideals—in the very makeup of their souls. And they were pair-bonded. Forever.

Before she might cry, Claire tried to lose herself in cleaning the room, slowed by her arm and distracted by her worry. No matter how she scrubbed, nothing seemed clean enough. But the worm was pulsing, indulging in her crazy behavior, whispering to her of how perfect this was, of the beauty of that grey-walled room, of the prowess of her mate and how clever he was in retrieving her.

By the time Shepherd arrived, Claire was resigned, sitting at the table with her head on her arms. Her mate had a tray for her, and looked over the room with approval upon finding that his female had occupied her time practically. They did not speak. Claire simply sat up, pushing her hair behind her ear, and frowned at the food.

It was a beautifully arranged chicken breast, drenched in a savory sauce thick with mushrooms and garlic. Exactly the kind of cuisine Claire loved, but something about the smell was off. It had been difficult to eat during those last few days of freedom, a side effect of fighting the bond, and she felt uncomfortable even as she reached for her fork. The man was purring, he smelled of rich Alpha, all things that should have brought her comfort, all things her body and mind had demanded when she'd been in hiding. Even so, she could hardly force half of the dish down.

It should have been good. She should have been hungry.

Feeling unwell, Claire pushed the food away and felt she might vomit. He stood beside her, reached down to pick up the customary vitamin she tended to forget, and waited for her to take it. Eager to just get it over with, she tossed it into her mouth and gulped the water. When it was done, when the pill had squirmed down her throat, she began to gag.

A warm hand came to the back of her neck and pushed her head between her knees, the purr increasing in volume and strength. The wave of nausea passed, but left her in a cold sweat. It had to be the stress, or maybe she'd picked up a bug. All Claire knew was that there was no fucking way she was swallowing another thing.

"I must check your claiming mark for signs of infection." It was not a suggestion, it was a command, and she knew it.

"Can you just give me a minute?" Claire grumbled, doubled over and not at all eager to straighten.

"I will retrieve what is required. It will take several minutes, which you may use to collect yourself."

The weight of his hand left her neck and Claire watched his boots disappear. Sucking in slow, cooling breaths, she managed to uncurl and wiped the sweat off her face with her forearm. By the time he returned, she'd lolled back in the chair, staring at the familiar concrete ceiling, still feeling like shit.

The beast approached. "Sit up straight."

A new tray was set down, filled with various medical instruments and two prefilled syringes. Eyeballing the strange assortment, Claire tensed when Shepherd slid the strap of her dress down. The gauze was pulled carefully away. Swabs soaked in hydrogen peroxide ran cool over hot skin, making the angry bite fizz. She looked away, unsure if she was going to puke. Everything he was doing seemed to be as concise as possible, to minimize discomfort, the hulk bending down and handling her gently.

She sat still through all the poking and prodding, extremely unhappy with the event, and just about ready to lose her cool and hide in the bathroom. Ointment was smeared over the mess, fresh gauze taped down, and then he stuck a digital thermometer in her ear and nodded at the result.

When those large hands went to grab one of the syringes, Claire stiffened and asked quickly, "What are those?"

"This is an antibiotic." Shepherd held her arm as if she might yank it away and injected her quickly. Claire watched the needle leave her skin, a tiny bead of blood welling. When he came at her with the second one, his grip tightened and he stabbed it much harder into the meaty part of her bicep. While she gave an irritated ouch, he pushed in the plunger and said frankly, "And this is a much purer form of the fertility drug you had in your pockets when you came to the courts."

"What?"

Claire was already shoving at him, beating at his arm with her fist to get him the hell off. The Alpha just ignored each blow and pressed a sterile cotton ball to the injection site, rubbing until her arm ached.

"YOU FUCKING BASTARD! HOW DARE YOU!"

Seemingly mellow, he explained, "That was your second dose. The first injection was administered upon your arrival twenty-four hours ago. That is why you feel ill."

The stomach acid, the cold sweat, the fever... it was exactly how she'd felt waiting in the courts, magnified by ten. Only this time, she was not terrified. Instead, she was about ready to kill him. While she screamed every obscenity she knew until red in the face, Shepherd simply held her arm and continued to knead the injected drugs into her muscle.

She was not due for another estrous for at least three months, five if she was lucky, and this jackass was forcing one on her.

"Why would you do this?" she spat at him. "Why?"

Without remorse, he explained, "Your body was too weak during your last heat to accept fertilization. You are stronger now. The chance of successful impregnation is much more likely."

"So you pump me full of drugs to breed me like a horse? Do you have any idea how fucked up that is? I have been pair-bonded to you for less than

137

two months. This is insane! And I would have cycled naturally in the spring!"

Shepherd spoke, completely unconcerned by her outburst, "Time is a factor, and as an Omega, motherhood will only bring you joy."

Claire was about to start tearing out her hair. "Shepherd, get the fuck out of this room! Take your poison and short-sighted assumptions about Omegas and LEAVE!"

When she saw laughter between his lashes, she lashed out and slapped him as hard as she could. All her violence accomplished was her stinging palm, Claire squeezing her fingers into a fist to cradle the offended digits to her chest. He seemed calm, as if completely expecting her tantrum, and stood through it as she railed and tried to get up from the chair.

When she was a disheveled mess, hair wild and eyes threatening murder, she felt another wave of horrible feverishness, worse than before, and growled like a beast. "I hate you!"

"You are hormonal."

Of course she was hormonal, he'd been pumping her full of hormones!

It came out from between tightly clenched teeth. "You are a pig... a bad mate."

"I guarantee that you will like me much better in a matter of hours," he cooed evilly, the backs of his fingers reaching out to stroke her cheek.

Claire jerked away and burst into tears. She didn't know if this was some sort of fucked up punishment or just another part of her life he had in his control. All she knew was that everything about what he'd done was not okay.

When he tried to pet her hair, she slapped his hand away and shrieked, "Don't touch me!"

She bent over, hid her face in her skirt, and sobbed. Shepherd stood by through the good ten minutes it took before her wailing distorted into gasping hiccups.

"If you will stop this crying, I will take you outside and show you your sky," he offered, his jeering replaced with subtle enticement.

She stayed bent, her face hidden, and slapped at the air in his direction. "Go to hell."

The thread, the little link between them, had been so happy, so full and warm, only an hour before, but now the thread was only pain, like a razor blade in her chest. She hoped to god it hurt him as much as it was hurting her, that the damn greasy cord was a two-way sense of torture. But then she remembered that he was only a psychopath with no heart, incapable of human emotion... that he was torturing Thólos on purpose.

Thinking about her mother, Claire understood everything that must have been going through that woman's head all those years... eating away at her until she just couldn't take it anymore. Her father may have been a decent man, but even Claire could see that her mother had not wanted him... that she'd longed for the female Alpha next door that she could never have. How freeing her suicide must have been. Control of her destiny, of the one thing the pair-bond wielding Alpha could not decide for her. The idea was growing increasingly appealing.

"I do not approve of the direction of your thoughts," Shepherd growled, low and threatening.

Claire ignored him.

Large hands circled her arms and pulled her up to stand. Refusing to look at him, she sniffed and turned her head, staring pathetically at the far wall.

"We will go outside. You will see your sky and you will feel better." It was a command. "This emotional response from the medication will pass."

It was like he had no idea how people worked.

All the signs of a steadily encroaching heat cycle were there: trembling shivers, cold sweat, her digestive tract shutting down. All the cleaning, the need for the room to be ready... Shepherd was right. In a few hours she would be begging him to fuck her.

Covering her mouth, another wave of nausea came.

He let her go, watching as she ran to the bathroom to vomit. Between her stomach vacating retches, she distantly recognized that he was holding back her hair, that his hand was stroking her back. Everything she had eaten was expelled until nothing but bile came up. She felt so utterly sick and so completely debased, sitting there on her knees with the very cause of her torment the facsimile of comfort.

"Why are you doing this?" she breathed, even as he wiped a cool towel over her face.

"I desire offspring. A legacy."

"You're sick." Rational thought was returning and Claire struggled to crawl out of the cradle of his lap so she might reach the sink and rinse out her mouth. "Even you must see that this is no place for a child."

He spoke with assurance, watching her brush her teeth and looming far closer than was comfortable. "Pregnancy will calm you into the rightful state of mind. There is no need for you to be upset, little one. I will provide you both with safety and comfort."

Spitting, she snarled, "Safety? You just poisoned me. Comfort? I live in a concrete box!"

His deeply warning silver eyes narrowed, Shepherd was clearly losing patience. "It was necessary, and it will only be beneficial to you if, in your coming estrous cycle, you should conceive."

"Do not make it sound as if your actions benefit me. I would be completely at your mercy. Pregnancy would make me actually need you!"

"You are already completely at my mercy. No more sulking." He took her by the scruff of the neck, the purr he'd incessantly offered never wavering as walked her back into the bedroom. "We will walk now."

Claire was not stupid. "Don't pretend this is an act of kindness. You want me to leave the room so others can come in and prepare it."

"You are very clever, little one. A good trait for the mother of my progeny."

"And you are very evil," she answered back, eyeing the mountain before her with abject loathing.

Shepherd seemed to grow, to spread out into the dim darkness of her prison. "I can be. But I am also a man, and I expect a child from the one I chose as mate. It is unfortunate the timeline does not please you, but it is what I wish." A large palm was extended for her to take, not exactly an act of politeness, and not exactly a threat. "Now come. I will escort you outside."

Claire had no coat and no shoes, so Shepherd wrapped her in a blanket, wiped her face and smoothed her hair, purring loudly to keep her from snarling. There was absolutely no one in the halls he led her through, as if he had prepared and ordered off any men who might have encountered the Omega who belonged to him. Walking the labyrinth, Claire memorized every turn, each little landmark, building a map in her head, ready to bolt at the first opportunity. Through it all, Shepherd maintained an unrelenting clamp on her hand. She wasn't going anywhere.

Their silent journey ended at the lower terrace, near the base of the Citadel—a disappointing segment which offered little in terms of the view beyond the fog-coated Lower Reaches. The blue-eyed Beta was there, armed and staring straight ahead, but no one else.

Feet freezing against the ground, a stiff wind pressed the fabric of the blanket against her legs, all discomfort was ignored by the unhappy Omega. Though it was dark, there was an expanse of sky far above, surrounded by towers reaching up to brush the top of the Dome.

If she squinted, she might make out the stars.

Claire ached, her heart a deep-seated, rotting piece of meat encased in ribs damaged by the worming thread. Absently, she began to rub at the spot, staring through tears, sick, and nearing hopelessness.

Shepherd stood behind her, flush to offer body heat, toying with her hair as it blew in the gusts. Every part of her longed to shove him away, to pull her hair from his fingers, but she knew that screaming at him in a rage in the room was the extent of the disobedience Shepherd would allow. Challenging him in front of a male, his subordinate Follower, would not end well for her. He had so much more to threaten her with now that chemically induced estrous approached. If she pushed him hard enough, he might go so far as to let his men mount her, and she was terrified at the thought of being shared like a whore.

A torment was coming. She was young, fertile, and Shepherd's scent advertised virile male. They were extremely biologically compatible. He would create life within her. As if it were already an actuality, Claire looked down to her flat belly and pressed her hand to where, in less than a week, a baby would be growing.

His nose was at the back of her skull, Shepherd breathing deeply. "You are feeling better."

"Does it matter how I feel?" she asked, low enough that her words were kept between them.

Tugging gently on her hair exactly the way he knew would calm her best, he answered, "It matters."

"I will never forgive you for this."

The man purred louder, his arm slipping about her middle like an anchor.

Turning around, eyes level with his chest, Claire put her hand on the relative part of his body where her own worming thread was hooked. Lifting wet, spiky lashes to look into expressionless silver eyes, she openly wept. "This is where you are tied to me, where the bond is threaded. Perhaps you are incapable of feeling what you've done, but I do know this: pair-bonded Alphas are supposed to care for their Omegas. But you do not... so why pair-bond to me? If all you wanted was a child, you could have injected me with your drugs and seeded me just the same. Why make me carry the burden of an unfulfilling bond? Why ruin me so I might never be happy?"

He did not look away, but she got the feeling he was trying to look through her. After the space of three breaths, Shepherd spoke. "You are young and believe that you understand the world from your short-sighted, idealistic perspective. You think you know much more than you do," he explained as if he were some great eloquent teacher, the music of his voice unaffected by the wind. "Sometimes, it is as unsophisticated as a man simply wanting to because he could, saw a chance, and took it."

The giant was talking in circles, giving her nothing at all. Claire took her hand from the place where she hoped he might feel something—some hint

144

of regret, something for her beyond the idea of a possession. "I will fight estrous."

"You will try." A finger hooked her chin and brought her attention higher. He was serious, his expression conveying his point. "But I am your mate, and I will see you through this heat. I will tend you and give you pleasure, and when it is finished, you will give me what I desire."

"If I fail to conceive, will you drug me again?"

Tucking back a strand of her hair, he nodded and softly answered, "Yes."

Locked in that silver gaze, Claire muttered, lost and shaken, "My feet are cold."

"I am aware, but I want you to experience your sky for as long as you can." He rubbed her back as if to warm her and continued almost gently, "We both know you cannot be trusted, little one. Therefore, you will not be seeing it again for quite some time."

A large warm thumb was already there to wipe away the angry tears he knew would fall at his verdict.

***

Corday pressed his back to the wall behind him and tried to ignore the chemically induced begging of the women locked in the room at his back. Only six Beta Enforcers had been allowed to remain on scene at the safe house, rotating who had to enter the room to force-feed the Omegas heat-suppressants every four hours. They did what they could to block out the pheromones, wore masks drenched in pungent oil, moved as quickly as possible. Even so, it set the Betas into the rut and each man had been tested. Two had been dragged outside to breathe clean air when whoever was watching through the pane of glass saw the change come over their comrade.

It was not intentional, and not one of the women had been touched. The compulsion was simply an act of nature they prepared for with checks and balances. The Enforcers tending to the Omegas worked as a team for that very reason. But even with their careful nursing, one of the females—a body that was little more than skin and bones—had already died from lack of nutrition and unseen internal injuries.

No one knew what her name was when they buried her in an overgrown terrace lawn, as deep as they could dig before hitting structure. Her story was unknown, another Jane Doe left to rot by Shepherd's occupation. The Omega had dark hair like Claire, a similar small frame. As the dirt had been laid over her, Corday felt sick, had almost cried, and went back inside before it was done, unable to look any longer.

Twelve hours had passed since the Omegas' first dose. Through the small window, Corday could see the sky had grown dark and braced himself. He would be next to enter the room reeking of chemically exaggerated estrous.

An alarm beeped, and the Enforcer who would watch over him as he shoved medicine into the women's mouths said, "It's time, man."

Nodding, Corday stood, took the offered mask they'd drenched in stink, then grabbed the pills and water. The door was opened and he moved forward, unconsciously holding his breath to start from left to right.

Their jaws opened willingly to suck his fingers. It was getting them to swallow that was almost impossible. He had to purr brokenly, which forced him to breathe, and practically drown them until they managed to swallow the pill. He made it through all five, felt the fever, and backed away even as his cock began to throb so hard it hurt. Once outside the room, he practically ran outdoors, his mind full of Claire and the moment of weakness he'd had at the apartment when the bathroom had smelled so damn good and had made him so fucking hard.

The fact that, even at that moment, he wanted to reach into his slacks and jack off, filled him with self-loathing. Corday fought it, stood in the cold for over an hour... just as all the other Enforcers who had been in the room had. Eventually, he found himself, grew flaccid, and went back inside to continue his watch. He prayed to the god of the Betas that he would not have to go back into that room.

The prayer, like all his others, was not answered.

It took almost three full days for the Omegas to come out of estrous, and five more trips into the pheromone-laced hell for Corday. As the females came to their senses, they were confused and scared... most having been so high they hardly remembered what had happened to them. The ones who did

147

remember were inconsolable or blank—like dolls with nothing inside. The Enforcers gave them food, each man assigned shifts for suicide watch.

Another Omega died by morning, the most vacant one... cause unknown. It was Brigadier Dane who sighed and said it seemed like the girl had just decided to stop breathing.

Corday buried her, knowing at least that her name was Kim Pham, right next to Jane Doe. That time, he cried like a baby.

Chapter 9

As they stood on the terrace, Claire suffered the first stirrings, the first warning sign it was time to fight estrous. A wave of warmth banished the cold, the blanket around her became uncomfortably hot, itchy... she tried to hide it. Her attempt to feign normalcy made no difference. Shepherd sensed the change at once. Without a word, she was lifted and swiftly carried back to her cage. Once the door was locked, she scampered off, forcing space between them, where she began pacing back and forth. Her march continued for hours, her stomach sour, her mood foul. The male seemed content to let her wring her hands and pace to and fro, noting she refused to even glance in the direction of the provided nesting materials, or at the table full of food prepared to see him through what might be a lengthy seclusion.

The knots in her gut twinged and soon she was breathing hard, pressing her hand to her belly, worried what his drugs were doing to a body nowhere near ready to ovulate.

A calming, muted voice came from the corner. "The discomfort will pass. There will be no long-term damage."

Claire threw the unwelcome presence a long, vicious growl, hating how he spoke as if he could read her mind. He ignored her disrespect, merely sitting like a gargoyle too big for his chair.

It was infuriating.

She wanted him to leave the room, unaccustomed to being near a male in those uncomfortable moments of pre-estrous. Forcing herself to ignore the intruder, Claire employed a catalog of tricks she'd learned over the years, small distractions that might ease the madness. Feverish, she found her hands in her hair. She braided her locks, paced, unbraided, breathed—over and over. The delicious smell in the air—the scent of a far too near Alpha—she pretended was something else: orange blossoms from the orchards her dad loved to visit. Every summer of her childhood, he'd purchased family admission to the highest level of the Gallery Tower so she could play in the dirt as little girls had once played before humanity retreated under glass for survival.

Each precious weekend had cost her father a month's wages.

Needing to crack her neck, her bones growing looser, Claire absently rolled her damaged shoulder. Instant pain stopped all movement. She'd forgotten. Looking down at the bandage, she trilled her fingers over the gauze. It hurt much less. Muted pain receptors signaled that full estrous was almost at hand.

Fear sharpened a clouding mind. Claire forced more thoughts of orange blossoms, ignored the need to pop joints, and tugged at her hair.

But time marched just as she did. Movements that had begun in a brooding, stiff cadence grew into something languid. Frustration spiked, diminished, leveled. And no matter how hard she tried to concentrate, her thoughts grew muddled.

At the sound of a purr, Claire began absently humming. Something soft came under her touch. Bedding, all fluffy, all new, lay in her arms. Once she realized she had mindlessly begun organizing the nest, she dropped it all, scattering the temptation, and stumbled back as if burned.

Shepherd chuckled. "You are doing fairly well, little one, but you will not last much longer."

Her head turned slowly toward the unwanted presence. Finding Shepherd naked, Claire's thought process slammed to a stop, her attention drawn to the bulging grandeur of his stiff cock.

Green eyes began to dilate.

The Omega had endured remarkably. She had denied and ignored him with a will deserving admiration. But there would be no more time wasted. Based on her behavior, Claire's reaction to the injection was stronger than predicted, her temper and outright aggression almost cute as she fell further in. Shepherd had found himself watching, hypnotized, as she sang under her breath and muttered about fields of orange trees.

"Come to me," he beckoned gently. "Let's end the charade. Allow your mate to tend to you."

She spat, measuring him as if she were the greater dynamic, "What, so I can kneel at your feet, Alpha? No!"

When the beast began to stand, to look at her as one looks at prey, the angry Omega stood her ground, showing teeth.

As he approached, she held her breath, determined to make a point that she could resist his scent and presence. Claire could prevail.

Shepherd went to his knees, purring beautifully and stroking her hips. His nose found the apex of her thighs, the heat of his breath hypnotic. "Is this what you wish, for me to kneel to you?"

His nearness exacerbated the internal chemical issue she had been fighting so well. Watching him, knowing he had approached, had knelt, to further his agenda, Claire whimpered. Standing rigid and uncomfortable, she fought the urge to touch him so hard, her muscles shook.

"Your eyes look very beautiful this way, little one," Shepherd crooned, mesmerized by the green irises slowly conquered by the encroaching black of her pupils.

He was not holding her. She could just walk away. One step, then another—it would be simple. Instead she grimaced, feeling that first sharp cramp of estrous slick. He smelled it at once and silver eyes flared. Rising with a flowing grace, Shepherd rubbed against her, pulling her dress in a swish of fabric over her head.

From the Alpha's chest came a demanding growl, the male relishing the way his mate's body doubled over at his call. For hours he had controlled his need to posture and pace so that she could have her short-lived victory. He had tested himself instead of descending into the rut and forcing her along. Now slick openly dripped down her legs. Now every fiber of his being needed to fuck her.

Shepherd wrapped a hand around the scruff of Claire's neck and pressed her lower. Fisting his cock, he rubbed the head of his manhood against her lips, spreading the heady fluid created to entice her into the frenzy. She stiffened, panted, the tip of her tongue flicking out against her will.

Swallowing, she keened.

"Is it not better when you don't fight what you are?" he asked, smoothing her black hair to expose hollowed cheeks to his view, hungry to watch her suck at his cock.

For a moment Claire remembered herself. On her knees, debased before him, Shepherd's cock slipped out of her lips and she looked as if she might weep. "What you have done is wrong."

The pads of his fingers burrowed against her scalp. "I am giving you life."

Unable to stop running her nose over the heat of his groin, she panted, "I already had a life. You destroyed it."

Feeling the fury, lust, and vehemence blend with wretched need, Claire clawed her way up his body. Dilated eyes wide and burning, she growled at the male. The noise had hardly left her throat before Shepherd spun her about and pressed her back into the mattress.

Arched, struggling to sheath the mountain cramming his throbbing cock into the pussy that wept for him, Claire entered full estrous. The cord was plucked to harmony, her insides eager for that first true sip of what her pair-bonded mate promised to give. Shepherd hooked her legs over his arms, allowed her to scratch and cling as he attacked, ramming fast and deep, staring into blown pupils while his little one howled.

He had enjoyed her during the Omega's first heat, but something was far more fulfilling in this second estrous cycle. Shepherd was as high on her pheromones as she was on his, knotting her with shouted roars each time her pussy clamped down and wrung his cock for fluids. Words were spoken they could hardly remember, shrieks of ecstasy and feral violence. Claire was so much stronger than before— nothing compared to him, of course, but she had no reservations about attacking if he did not please her. And Shepherd loved it, loved how he had to pin her down, secure viciousness, and overtake his prey.

Claire slept in spurts, always lying on top of him, no matter how he tried to tuck her against his side. When she woke the first time, she looked down at the mess of blankets and just knew they were all wrong. Shoving at the warm mass in her way, she snarled until it shifted, yanking soft materials out from under the Alpha.

As she designed the nest, the heat of a nearby body lingered at her side. Shepherd sniffed her often, running his fingers through the dripping fluids that ran sluggishly down her thighs, stopping only to hand the Omega pillows or whatever she demanded next. When it was done, Claire pushed him back into what she had built and took what she wanted—a thing she had never done before. Riding his cock at her pace, watching him and relishing the way he eased that horrible internal itch, she came powerfully, loving the look in his eyes when she grinned.

The Omega prowled over him, her black eyes utterly absorbed in his body. It kept him hard for days. When she grew tamer, as the overblown reaction to forced estrous lessened, she would stay still long enough for him to scent her, for his big hands to rub the puddle of come that had leaked out of her womb all over her skin, to feed it to her as he purred and gave affection.

When her high was near its end, Shepherd moved in her gently, his silver eyes watching every tick, seeing that she smiled softly and gasped in pleasure with each thrust. He put his lips on hers.

Even caught in estrous, she repeatedly refused his kiss.

Shepherd found it very displeasing.

With her small, conquered, exhausted, and distracted in orgasm, it would be so simple to take... but he needed her to come so he might knot her. He needed her to cry out—because once she did, once he had her fully trapped where she could not resist, he was going to force what was his due.

Eager for his due reward, his hips snapped, he clutched her too tight. Mouth at her ear, Shepherd howled, "COME NOW!"

Something in his tone, the absolute command, and Claire spasmed. Eyes rolling back in her head, her climax crashed too soon and too hard. Shepherd's knot swelled huge behind her pelvic bone, the beast groaning loudly with each gush. With her mouth open in a silent scream, he took advantage. Shackling hands held her in place, as if the female would panic. His rough lips crashed down.

She tried to turn her head, body twisting. No matter how he teased her tongue, how he sucked her lips, Claire would not engage.

Issuing another stream of semen into his Omega, Shepherd lifted his head and found her eyes hooded, distant. Growling, frustrated, he demanded, "Kiss me, little one."

Full lips came again to hers. When Claire locked her teeth, he grabbed her jaw and brought her face back to his. "Look at me."

It was the rough-hewn voice that broke through the haze of orgasm, Shepherd desperate and almost human. She glanced at the source, confused. A ragged scar ran diagonally across what was still a beautiful mouth. She found a strong jaw. She looked at him as if for the first time, studied the Alpha who had taken her, who had drugged her to force a child into her womb—the one whose purrs almost brought her as much peace as the sky.

"Look at the man you claim to hate," snarled words were distorted by gnashing teeth, "and kiss me, little one."

Claire continue to stare, reaching up to touch, to trace the lines of her mate's face—the stubble on his jaw, his fine nose, and the aggressive lips with their arresting scar. She whispered to him. The great beast began to tremble, eyes clouding with what almost looked like physical pain.

She did not offer her lips, but she pulled his head to her breast and offered a tingling nipple instead. He sucked greedily.

***

Tucked against him, his Omega slept far more deeply than she had after he'd broken her previous heat cycle. Carefully running his fingers through the dark mass of her hair, Shepherd purred, just as possessive as he had been from the first. Obsessive thoughts circled in his head, centered on the female in his care, on how to keep her, on how to continue. She was his. He was never going to share her. She'd stay in this room and he would pet and purr as much as was needed while the child he'd planted grew.

What was a sky compared to that? Nothing. The sky was nothing.

His little one stirred, and dark lashes fluttered open. Seeing his face, smelling the familiarity of his breath, Claire hummed sadly and put a hand to her belly. "I am pregnant."

"You are, little one. Your scent is already altering." He disregarded the look in her eyes when it was not exactly one of joy, and stroked her cheek. "You will provide me with a fine child."

Something about the way he spoke made her incredibly uneasy. The haze of lust was gone. The moments of tender words and untrustworthy proclamations passed. Automatically, the purr increased and the tugs on her hair resumed. Watching him with distrust, Claire filtered through the memory of the last few days, aware he had been patient with her initial refusal and outright drug-induced aggression. Shepherd could have debased her, but for hours he'd simply watched—until she began to drip, until the rut became unavoidable. Not that it absolved him of what he'd done, the manipulative bastard. She almost wished he would have just outright raped her.

He'd got what he wanted without her consent or approval, and been rewarded with a very willing bedmate in estrous.

"Are you going to keep our child locked in this room, too?" she asked, nervous that no matter what his answer was, it would not be good enough.

"No." The purr came full force.

Claire reached for his hand, holding his eyes as she pulled the roughened palm down her sticky body where it might rest over the life planted within her. It was almost impossible to bring herself to whisper, "Will you separate me from..."

The hand on her abdomen tightened over a womb cradling rapidly dividing cells, owning their combined genetics. "You do not need to worry over such things."

"That is not an answer." She rose to an elbow, growing indignant. "I was not ready for a child—certainly not with a man I hardly know—but you have done this, and I would know what you are going to do to us."

"Already the protective Omega mother. I find that pleases me." There was a strange glow in his eyes, as if the bastard was grinning, though his scarred lips remained neutral. Pressing her down into their nest, he purred, "I will not part you from our child."

But would somebody else? The man had ways of spouting half-truths. "Shepherd." The name was spoken like a threat.

There was a smile in his voice, a hint of something dark, as well. "Yes, little one?"

"Do not give me cause to hate you more."

He was charmed by the warning, and began to twist his fingers in a long strand of midnight hair. "No more talk of hatred. You are my mate, bound, and you will devote yourself to me."

Dark brows shot up and her jaw dropped. "You cannot force that."

The pad of his thumb traced her lips. "I can."

As if in agreement with the man, the thread began to bang loudly in her chest. There was to be no more talk, she was too tired to argue. The familiar weight of his hand moved from her belly to between her legs. Ignoring how Claire turned her head away, he began to stroke the little bundle of nerves, flicking it to entice it to swell.

Shepherd growled and purred as he played with her pussy. "Submit. I will be gentle and you will enjoy it. Once you are calm, you will sleep more."

***

The room was colder than the cell Nona had been locked in for the past six days. A guard, a brutish man four times her size, gestured to the empty chair across from a Beta she had seen on the premises. That Beta had led the men who'd dragged Lilian and her friends away days ago.

"My name is Jules. Take the seat, Nona French."

He had an unplaceable inflection and the startling blue eyes of a bully. She knew his type. Nona pulled out the chair.

"Your registration states you are a Beta, and according to your clearly fraudulent record, you have never been pair-bonded or conceived children," the man began, looking up from the file before him to meet the older woman's eyes. "Are you the one who taught Miss O'Donnell to live as a Beta?"

The woman had her own questions and was disinterested in the Follower's bullshit. "Where is Claire?"

The smallest of smirks came to the Beta's face. Placing his hands on the table, he took his time organizing his body into a position of subtle intimidation. "She is where she belongs. With her mate."

"The Alpha, Shepherd?" It was asked like a question, but they both knew it was a statement of disgust. She'd seen the brute carry her off, Nona spraining her wrist trying to fight free so she might

160

save her. Her wrinkled lips turned down at the corner, and the old woman's hands mirrored his—a strangely antagonistic stance for an Omega. "He locked her in a room for five weeks. That is no proper mate."

Hard, unblinking eyes held hers. Jules clarified, "Seclusion is customary behavior when adjusting one's Omega into their new life."

She laughed right in his face. "I should not be surprised at your lack of civility, given what you are. No wonder she was too ashamed to admit who had claimed her. Does he beat her, too?"

"When you saw her, did she look beaten?" The man leered, leaning forward.

Nona answered calmly. "She looked terrified and unwell."

"How long have you known Miss O'Donnell?"

The severe-faced woman said nothing.

Jules was through playing games. "It is in your best interest to answer my questions, Ms. French."

"Or what? You'll lock me in jail so that I can be given away at my next estrous?"

"At your age, estrous would be unlikely. I would simply have you killed."

Tapping her fingers on the table, Nona smiled. "I'm old. And I lived on my terms. The threat of death does not overly concern me."

"What about torture?"

"Only one way to find out."

161

Jules smiled and leaned back in his chair. "I didn't say your torture. There are two Omegas in our custody too young to serve a purpose. It is them I will torture if you do not tell me what I want to know."

Nona's anxiety spiked. Lips pressed in a line, she nodded.

Looking back at the file, Jules began again. "How long have you known Miss O'Donnell?"

Her answer was vague. "We were introduced two years before her mother died."

"And you have been a surrogate parent?"

"I have been a friend," Nona grunted. "Claire is independent and did not need to be coddled."

Jules looked to her again. "So she is not aware that, when her father died, you funded the endowment that allowed her to pursue art over menial labor?"

"She is not," Nona answered, her lips tight. "As far as I knew, only the bank had access to such information."

Suddenly the tenor of the conversation altered. The air grew thick and Jules spoke with no smile or intonation. "It seems you have a strong personal attachment to the girl, which makes me wonder why you allowed her to enter the Citadel."

A deep furrow grew between Nona's brows. "We both volunteered, but I was supposed to be the one to go to the Citadel."

"Explain."

"She stole the prepared clothing while I was bathing. By the time I was aware of what had happened, she was gone. Claire is very protective of the ones she loves."

"Did no one try to stop her?"

"The group agreed with her reasoning." The woman looked away, her disappointment obvious. "And many simply thought she would be more appealing as our representative. It was a very close vote."

"Is that not ironic?" Bored, the man looked her dead in the eye. "Who was her contact to Senator Kantor?"

"Since you have already questioned the women who met with her that evening, I am certain you are aware that it was never mentioned in the brief conversation we shared." Leaning on her elbows, the older woman demanded, "I want to see Claire."

"No," the Beta answered flatly.

The interrogation continued, a list of assorted questions about Claire's history, her quirks—some so precise, such as her favorite fruit, that even Nona did not know the answer. The exchange was strange, and she wondered why Shepherd did not ask Claire these questions himself.

***

There had been only exhaustion in Claire's short-lived freedom, and Shepherd had allowed her no rest upon her return. Between the eight days of insomnia and the chemical alertness of estrous, Claire was drained in a way she had never known. There was never enough sleep. Her former restlessness was replaced with haunting lethargy and an unwillingness to move from the nest. When she woke, she would be burrowed, completely covered. Once or twice, she snarled at the male reaching in to pluck her out from under all the covers so she might eat or he might dress her wound.

All she wanted was the dark and to be left alone. But Shepherd would appear no matter how much she hated the sight of him, the man dragging her to stiffly lie atop him. Too tired to complain, she lay limp, knowing he would cover them both and reproduce her burrow. Once total darkness returned, she would pretend the bastard was not there... or she would try. Shepherd would only let her rest for a short time before his seeking hands more than petted the lingering soreness from her body, fondling increasingly tender breasts and playing between her legs.

Claire did not want the attention, hated that his smell did things to her, that she craved it so badly she had a need to burrow into his side of the bed when he was gone. As if he knew what kept her constantly sniffing him, yesterday's shirts began to appear in their nest. Upon waking, finding them pressed to her nose, Claire would toss them out and curse him to hell.

Shepherd would put them back when he returned.

It was almost a game. That morning, Shepherd raised the stakes. Claire threw one out and woke to find two in its place. When she realized what he'd done, she giggled, a sound that made the secret observer in the corner perk his ears, never having heard her sound for joy. Unaware she had an audience, she threw his things on the floor and burrowed deeper, still laughing.

There was a swat on her rump, and she shrieked in surprise. Twisting, shoving the blankets off her head, Claire sat up, hair a mess, and found him standing over the bed, demonstrably dropping the clothing in her lap.

At the blush on her cheeks, Shepherd was the one chuckling, prowling over her to sniff at the bedraggled woman. "You think your rejection of your mate's scent in this nest is funny?"

She had not spoken to him—even to ask the hour—in days. Too tired, too confused, still angry, she frowned, unsure of his tone or intention.

"Is your protest a silent way to communicate your preference for the real thing?"

It seemed almost as if he was flirting. Claire cocked a brow, croaking, "No."

Shepherd fisted the blankets and drew them over their heads, pulling her against him as he rebuilt her burrow. Settling back, hating that he was not taking the proper position, and instead looming over her, Claire felt his hand move between them. His fist was pumping, and it took her a minute to realize that he was stroking his cock. A few small grunts, a warning growl when she tried to move away, and his hand moved faster until he groaned low and long. Splashes bathed her naked belly and breasts, fluid pooling until it dripped into the nest and scented the confined space far more strongly than any used shirt.

As if she was in estrous, he rubbed it into her skin, pressed it between her resistant lips, and made sure his seed got everywhere. Something about the act, that he'd done it for his own pleasure and none of hers, left her feeling neglected. He left her as soon as his scenting was done, Claire frowning at his back. Peeking out from her burrow, it took mere minutes before she was tempted to exchange the darkness of her blankets for the subterranean dimness of her cage.

Her bare feet padded silently to the dresser, green eyes sneaking a glance at the Alpha working at his COMscreen. Dressing, oblivious she lacked an urge to wash his semen away, Claire began to do what she usually did in her waking hours underground; she paced. Her joints were stiff from so much sleeping, and the walking did little to ease her black mood.

Shepherd seemed content to ignore her. She was trying to ignore him, but as the hour progressed, she began unconsciously edging a little bit nearer.

Staring, Claire found his COMscreen bizarre and unreadable. Sighing, bored, she popped her lips and yipped when a great arm swooped out and snatched her out of the blue. Once she was tucked across his lap, Shepherd went right back to whatever he had been doing, trapping her in a cage of overly muscled limbs.

She had been so quiet and he had seemed so focused. It had not been her intention to invite interaction. She squirmed against his chest. "I'm hungry."

An answer came. "No you're not. You're restless and desire attention."

What she was, was irritated. "Why aren't you purring?" The jerk could at least do that. For fuck's sake, it was the only thing he was good for.

Claire could not prove it, but she was fairly certain he was laughing at her, despite his silence. "If I purred, you would not have been coaxed nearer."

Rubbing at the soreness in her shoulder, she narrowed her eyes.

Smirking, he went on, "Your mood swings are mildly amusing, little one."

"What is this?" She gestured toward the screen, unwilling to be baited, and far more willing to be aggravating.

His attention went back to his work. "If you were meant to read it, it would be in your language."

Claire simply rolled her eyes. Lesson learned. She would pointedly keep her distance to avoid this situation in the future.

"No, you won't."

When he responded to private thoughts that were none of his business, she snapped, "Stop doing that!"

Ignoring her, Shepherd's finger went to the screen and tapped until something new flashed, bright and pretty. Leaning forward, she eagerly reached out to take hold without thinking. He began to purr and she to smile as she looked at an image of her family.

"Your father was an Alpha." It was clear that that was who had all her attention in the photograph, that it was his face her finger ghosted over. "Your mother was an Omega."

Obviously...

Claire was trying to ignore the distracting man, to focus on something worthy, seeing the patch of blue sky in the background, as they all stood together in the orange grove.

"My mother didn't like my father," she taunted, pointing out the parallel to their situation.

Shepherd mocked her right back. "And to avoid her fate, you sequestered yourself away, became something unnatural."

Her dark head swung around to face the man who could not possibly understand. "There is nothing wrong with celibacy and self-control! You might think I am beneath you, but your short-sighted view of Omegas is pathetic and limiting. It shows very much what kind of mind stands behind the charisma and insane agenda. I made it years! Years, Shepherd. And you ruined everything."

Seeing the building fire in his eyes, Claire realize what she'd done. She grew nervous he would react to her outburst, and instinctively covered her belly to protect what was hidden inside.

His tone hissed a forced sort of neutral. "And what was this great plan you saw for yourself? How were you to find a mate when you lived in seclusion and behaved like a Beta?"

Defensive, she grumbled, "I was courted... on occasion."

Shepherd's tense physical response was clearly displeased. "Betas?"

"Betas respect my boundaries. Alphas are dangerous and take without asking."

"And you lied to them about your dynamic."

Scowling, Claire clarified, "I just didn't say anything about it. Being an Omega should not be what defines me, any more than the color of my skin or the level in which I was reared."

"Your mother's suicide had a strong impact on your thinking."

Claire shook her head and gave a cynical sigh, not at all surprised he had researched her history. "I find it funny how often in my life Alphas have tried to equate my subversive behavior with my mother's death. I am not the only Omega to feel this way—many of us do. And if you Alphas had a lick of sense, you would take time to talk to us instead of just spreading our legs for your own amusement."

"Was your father unkind to your mother?"

Claire looked back to the screen. "He doted on her, but it didn't matter. She was in love with someone else."

That stopped him at once. He began to gather her hair in his fist, pulling her head back to force her attention. "You will love no one but me."

Every feeling inside made her long to spit out the truth, to scream that she did not love him at all. But she could smell the aggression, the dominance and anger, and knew speaking was dangerous. Their conversation was at an end, the point driven home a moment later when his hand slipped under her skirt and the growl was made.

Chapter 10

Corday's assumption was accurate. Betrayal by those closest to Claire had allowed Shepherd to abduct his friend. Standing with the masses gathered before the Citadel, he watched three emaciated women being shoved forward to be gawked at and heckled by the crowd. The Omegas had been charged with theft and battery, Shepherd himself shouting their sentence as the terrified females were dragged, then propped up so each might have a noose fitted around her scrawny neck.

Tens of thousands had come to watch the sentencing, Dome Broadcasts having announced the upcoming executions for days.

Thólos Dome had once been the pinnacle of evolved human culture, maintained and exalted no matter the ruins left far behind and far away—the greatest of the Domes. Capital punishment had not existed before the breach. The worst male offenders were sent to the Undercroft, the females to the farming levels to labor. And now the city was enamored with such morbid pageantry, cheering for their conqueror, and hungry for blood.

It was an extravaganza, a visual warning to remind the population who was in charge. It was a sham.

Shepherd postulated, eloquent and captivating, listing the three Omegas' sins, calling them cowards and aggressors—rattling off a record of crimes so ridiculous Corday found the crowd's gasps preposterous. How could they not see what this was? Could they not grasp that those skeletal women were terrified and pleading... that they had been gagged so their shrieks would be nothing but noise?

Shepherd approached the Citadel's archway—turned into a macabre scaffold—large and terrible, the Da'rin markings on his arms flaunted as if the pain they caused him were nothing. The convicted Omegas sobbed pathetically, their eyes darting over the crowd in search of deliverance, mercy... anything.

"Lilian Hale, Xochitl Ramos, Barb Guppy, you have been found guilty and are sentenced to death by hanging."

Shepherd himself, the monster who had Claire in his possession, kicked each support from under the terrified females' feet. They fell—a short drop, their toes kicking a few inches from the ground. Through it all, Shepherd watched them jerk and thrash, fixated. Fifteen agonizing minutes passed before the last of the women stopped twitching.

The rabid crowd lost its edge when the women's uncovered faces turned grotesque shades of purple, the corpses' eyes bulging. Two of them had wet themselves and, in the end, it appeared as if Thólos recognized and began to suffer the fear Shepherd had intended to inspire. The three bodies were left there to swing in the breeze, exposed to the birds when Shepherd turned his back and walked away. The mob began to disperse.

With hands deep in his pockets, Corday moved on. Some part of him had hoped Shepherd would have Claire at his side, that he would flaunt her, though deep down such an idea was ridiculous.

But Corday needed to see her, to know she was okay. For her to see him, so she might know he was fighting for her.

There were so many unanswered questions, so much that weighed on his shoulders, and when he closed his eyes each night, it was her in that grave he saw being covered in dirt—Claire's green eyes, staring dead and unblinking at the sky, which haunted him.

Shepherd was a psychopath. It had been two weeks and Corday was not sure if his friend was even still alive. The temptation to approach, to ease just close enough to see whether he carried her scent, took Corday's feet up the steps and into the Citadel.

It was madness, he knew that. He had totally lost his mind. But with the crush, with the fanfare and the rowdy froth of the crowd, he was unseen and unnoticed. The stink of the room was intrinsically gross. With unwashed males and a few of the more nasty Alpha females, the air was laced with an aggressive musk that mingled into a pungent stench that would warn off the vulnerable and timid. Corday could imagine Claire walking into such a place, could see her being swallowed up.

She had claimed a riot broke out at the start of her heat, that Shepherd had killed a lot of people to claim her. If it was in the midst of this group, she was lucky they had not started ripping off her limbs.

But Shepherd had fought the mob for her...

That was the one part Corday still could not wrap his mind around. Shepherd was a killer, the type to enjoy the bloodbath. He'd just murdered three women. So why fight for Claire, why pair-bond?

Edging through the crowd, mimicking the savage behavior of those shouting for more, Corday went unnoticed. He only needed to get within fifteen feet before he smelled the scent Shepherd wore with pride. Claire's slick—Shepherd's trophy—was fresh, as if he'd only just had her before executing the Omegas Corday's gut told him were responsible for turning her over to the brute.

It was all too surreal, too double-edged. But Claire was alive. In that, Corday found reassurance. So he must remain strong for her—for all the oppressed—and he, like the other Enforcers, would find a way to end this madness.

Gritting his teeth, he left the Citadel.

**

Shepherd found her under her burrow again, fast asleep in a circle of his scented garments. His Omega was almost always sleeping, a side-effect of the early stages of pregnancy. Turning her into the curve of his body, he saw her grimace, draw in his scent, then come awake startled.

Pensive, she began to sniff at him, scowling deeper each time she did. It was impossible to miss her displeasure at whatever she found. Stranger still, she made no secret of her appraisal, climbing over him until her nose was breathing in the air exhaled from his mouth.

Revulsion sat thick in her eyes.

Shepherd let her climb out of bed to approach the bathroom, where he could hear her turn on the shower. Her new ploy, the extensive cold-shouldered silence, continued. Claire was not going to speak to him. She simply marched back in the room with her hand over her nose, her silent way of telling the Alpha to wash off the smell.

"Explain your issue," Shepherd growled, watching her grimace deepen.

Her tongue was sharp when she lowered her hand. "You stink of many hostile Alphas... you contaminated my nest."

He rose from the bed, narrowing his eyes at the disgust on her face. "Your tone is undesirable."

Claire wiped her face clean of her unfriendly expression, needing him to wash, refusing to give him a reason to fuck her while he smelled of the very squalid men who'd almost raped her in the Citadel.

Her heart picked up pace. An off note vibrated out of tune from her end of the thread. "Please don't touch me while you smell like… them."

The way she whispered the entreaty, the odd fear in her eyes, made him frown and skirt away from where she stood, pleading. Shepherd moved into the bathroom.

175

She stripped the bed in a flurry, bunching up all the offensive sheets to dump by the door. New, unsatisfactorily scentless bedding was put on at once.

Claire was already burrowed when he came back, smelling only of soap and Shepherd. His hand ran over her cloth-covered body. "Come out of there."

She twisted and sat up, finding the monolith naked at the side of the bed.

Piercing silver eyes dissected her trepidation. It was worded as a question and a lure. "Do you still find me offensive?"

In many ways, yes. "No."

He cocked a brow, challenging, "Are you certain? I do not wish to contaminate our nest."

Unwilling to invite negative attention, she moved to her knees to nose his stomach, hoping the action would satisfy him enough that he might leave her in peace. "You smell as you should."

It was another one of those new games of his, Shepherd's crafty ways of drawing her out, the manipulation to earn attention outside of her persistent anger. Climbing over her, arranging her body so their skins were flush, he reached for the covers and pulled them over their heads, recreating the soft, dark burrow she liked best.

Feeling her nose at his neck, hearing her absently sniff, it was clear his Omega was appeased—even humming her strange music, contented when his fingers started to manipulate the muscles along her spine. Soon enough, Claire was utterly tranquil, her soft breaths revealing slumber was a heartbeat away.

A rasping breath preceded, "What have you done in my absence?"

Half-asleep, she grumbled, "The same thing I am trying to do right now."

"I have other plans for you."

He felt her body tense, the Omega expecting to be manhandled. A catch of breath hitched before a tone devoid of emotion seemed to strangle her words. "I'm tired."

Correcting her, Shepherd flexed the arm strewn across her lower back and answered with his own low reassurance, "It is natural at this stage that your body feels lethargic while it adapts to its new task. This malaise will pass."

It seemed like such a predictable explanation for her reluctance.

Claire put her chin to his chest and glanced towards the man burrowed in her nest. He ran his palm up her body until it rested flush against her cheek. Watching her reaction, knowing she thought darkness concealed her, he found her expression was not grimaced in the miserable distrust he'd stomached since her return. Instead, it was softly rendered into a state of the resigned acquiescence she refused to show where she thought he might see it.

Taking time to trace her lips, to watch her close her eyes and find a moment's peace under his touch, Shepherd wondered aloud, "You are still angry with me for inducing estrous, even though you were well-cared for during and since."

Claire stiffened, her face forming back into a reflection of sadness. "I suspect you desire a specific answer. I am too drained to figure out what it is."

There had been little conversation between them in their short acquaintance. Most dialogue usually ended the instant Shepherd no longer found her replies acceptable. The frustration of fighting to be heard had passed into disillusioned acceptance. As things were, Claire possessed little interest in anything but sleep.

In that dark little tent of blankets, she looked towards the sound of his breath, chewing her lower lip and wishing that moments like these, the times he would seem gentle, were her reality, that the dark nameless warmth and male body was someone else.

Speaking through the purr he projected gently into her smaller body, he asked, "Beyond leaving the safety of this space, what would lessen this discontent?"

"A window."

Burrowing the pads of his fingers against her scalp, rubbing just enough so she'd close those unhappy eyes, all seemed so much better when his mate almost leaned into his hand. "There are several shelves of windows waiting across the room, which you have pointedly ignored."

"I don't need to learn how to be a dictator. I don't want to be anything like you."

Shepherd smiled. "I agree. You would make a terrible Follower and would require constant punishment for insubordination."

A palm cupped her face and brought it fractionally higher. His voice in the dark breathed, "You are smiling."

Was she? No, she could not have been. "And how do you punish your Followers?"

The pad of his thumb traced over her forced pout, Shepherd teasing, "Would you prefer corporal punishment over being physically attuned to your proper course?"

There was a stifled coughing noise, and Claire moved out of his palm and pressed her face to his chest. A shudder wracked her body, Shepherd feeling her lips curve against his skin. And then it escaped—a second burst of strangled laughter.

The purr returned in full force. "And now you are laughing..."

"Of course not." She cleared her throat, trying her damnedest to keep her lips from twitching.

The pads of his fingers skimmed her ribs. Claire flinched, stiffened, and then bit her lip to stop her forced, laughing shrieks. "Shepherd!"

"Yes?" He trilled his fingers over her flank as she shied and tried to slip away, only to be caught in all her blankets.

They twisted as he mercilessly tickled. All the while, Shepherd noting each slip, each little quake of a giggle to escape. He seemed alive, full of a new,

179

unusual energy as his ribs expanded and contracted above her in rapid, excited breaths. "Little one, you are alight again."

Automatically sucking her lower lip in her mouth, Claire grunted, "You're smashing your baby."

His weight shifted, and thin branching crow's feet developed outside his eyes as Shepherd observed the female trapped beneath him.

Scarred lips pressed to her neck, the behemoth sucked in a deep, rasping breath. "I favor you this way, little one."

His body flexed against her, and suddenly the massive killer was playful, setting his hip between hers. Immediately unsettled, Claire realized she had behaved badly in her fatigue. She had invited attention, she had engaged... and he seemed very happy about it. Taking her hand, he put her palm on his chest and drew it down the length of his torso, arching into the compelled touch like a spoiled cat.

Claire watched her fingers on their course, wondering idly if he even registered, or cared, that it was only his force on her wrist which continued the caress. She wondered if the thread spoke to him as it did to her. What manipulations was it working in his mind?

The ripple of knotted muscles over Shepherd's ribs, the hard line of his belly, so much mass and heat. Her eyes traveled up to find him watching her clinically, gauging her expression. The moment became far more confusing, as did the light furrow of his brow and the almost intrigued expression surrounding his liquid mercury eyes.

His body shifted, Shepherd drawing Claire's palm higher until it rested against the swirl of tattoos on his thick neck—the forefront of his Da'rin markings. He sniffed and growled low, releasing the pressure of his hand on hers. "I am sore here."

The beast stilled and waited, covering but not crushing her, his complaisance urging her only to stroke him. It seemed a reasonable thing, but she hesitated. Touching him in coitus while her mind was on another plane was one thing. Giving him relief simply because he wanted her to... she was resistant to offer it.

When his hand moved to her breast and began to knead the mound of flesh, Claire stiffened, bracing as she understood his point. His erection had been growing between their bodies and was already pulsing and ready. She could rub him, or he could fuck her.

He was giving her a choice.

Her small hand reached for the covers, to recreate the wrecked burrow, then her hand went back to the thickly muscled nape of his neck.

The beast released her breast, growling low and long at the feel of her hand kneading his spine.

The sensation of touching him seemed so very bizarre. Thinking of it as a chore, considering the act clinically, Claire let her hand recognize where there was tension in the musculature, where she could feel scars. The more she dug in, the deeper his purr became. It seemed the behemoth was nearing sleep, his weight settling a bit more atop her, but that was not what distracted Claire's attention. It was the still hard meat of his cock, and how it would jerk, as if Shepherd were flexing a muscle every so often, butting against her sex. Secondly, her breast, the one he'd caressed in the unspoken offer, was sensitive, and the nipple distended to the point where it ached. Claire had to take great care, as she rubbed Shepherd's neck, to ensure the mound of flesh did not come into contact with him, that the inappropriate thrill when the peaked nipple scraped heat was ignored.

It was maddening.

Even in the early stages of pregnancy, her body reacted to his nearness far more strongly than it had before. Where there had been disgust, Claire began to feel stirrings. It was only a physical reaction, but it felt like a betrayal of her very self when revulsion disappeared and her mind tried to shut off the torrent of endless internal reproofs.

That was why he'd done it, she was certain. Pregnancy made her crave the nearness of the father, almost inspired the interest Shepherd seemed to demand. A long worried breath passed her lips. The giant shifted just a little. As if some threshold had been crossed, some test finished, he seamlessly began to ease the head of his cock into her supine body. Claire pretended it was unwelcome even as she continued to stroke his neck.

She moaned.

Her expression hinted that she found his callused fingers distasteful, but the flush on her cheeks gave her away when slowly he returned his large hand to her swollen breast.

182

There was something under the surface of the act she could not put her finger on, something in the way the pad of his thumb circled her flesh, his cock still slowly pushing inside her, as if testing the waters. It was too much, as if he was waiting for some revelation, some great moment, and like a bucket of cold water Claire realized what had happened.

Shepherd had never made the growl.

There was no derision, no mocking of her confusion and instant panic, only the satin movement of his hips thrusting forth until her slick passage was filled to the brim. They shared breath. Shepherd rolled his hips, watching her eyes in the dark as Claire came to terms with what had led her to tremble. Her body had broadcast the scent of slick, and he had acted instantly to fulfill something her mind would have never allowed.

She had wanted him.

His warm fingertips left her breast to trace her lips, the line of her jaw, Shepherd watching her hooded green eyes close completely.

The seduction seemed organic—missing the measured calculation he usually employed—but Claire's mind was in turmoil, and she had to do something. It was like a flash of inspiration, the only way she could fight back, because his new dominance over her body had to stop somewhere. He might be drawing soft gasps and murmurs from her lips, but she had the power to think of another. At first it was almost easy, her little mental defiance. She thought of the one person she knew Shepherd hated, his unknown nemesis—she thought of Corday.

Like the flow of a river, Shepherd turned them both until her burrow fell away and he was holding her above him. There was no dark shelter where her face and feelings could hide, he had exposed her... but so long as her eyes remained closed, she could maintain defiance and pretend.

He rolled his hips even as he commanded her, "Little one, you will look at me when I fuck you."

The weight of his gaze drew her attention, and automatically the fan of her lashes lifted. Claire looked through passion drugged eyes. Green found shining silver. All thought disappeared, the image she'd tried to maintain vanished as if it had never existed. There was only Shepherd.

"Good girl."

Large hands lifted and lowered her hips, the pace still slow, Claire braced on his massive chest to do as she was compelled. Leaning into his touch, caught up, she sucked his fingers. Shepherd angled to hit the place she presented, drawing out her gasps until she began to keen softly. Being pleasured by the Alpha had always been a sensation of mind-bending carnality, but at that moment, all she could register was shining silver and soft touches. In combination with a long hum, her pussy twitched and clasped Shepherd's cock like a fist, drawing the Alpha deeper, enticing him to spill. He did, groaning as he yanked her writhing hips flush against his so he might knot deep in her core.

With the splash of heat in her belly, she was humming, contented. Shepherd pulled her closer, chest to chest, groaning long and loudly as another wave of come shot from his cock just as her pussy clenched for more.

They were locked together, and would be so for some time by the feel of it. With her cheek to the damp skin of his chest, Claire listened to his heart. At moments like that, the thread no longer seemed greasy. It seemed clean, and even when she pretended it was not there, it hummed, singing to her.

Painful self-loathing returned.

There was no comforting purr when her mind grew anxious, no pets to soothe her tension. Shepherd wanted her to recognize the quality of their exchange. Shifting as if to put distance between them, Claire felt the huge bulbous anchor hooked behind her pelvic bone reminding her resistance was pointless. Trapped, she tried to be still, to allow the waves of castigation to burn each and every vein.

In a voice almost laced with compassion, the male offered, "Your reaction was not unnatural."

It began to feel as if the whole thing had been planned, down to the very breath she drew to speak. "And your neck," she began in a voice full of self-hate, "does it still hurt?"

"Your touch eased the pain." Feeling her bury her face against him as if ashamed, he ceased the lesson and offered a purr, allowing his arms to come around her, to cradle her as she needed but could not ask for.

***

185

It was not much longer, perhaps only a handful of days, before Claire began to sleep less and to grow anxious when left alone. She no longer found joy in her hours of seclusion as she had before he'd infected her with poison. Instead, isolation left her edgy. When Shepherd was not present, time dragged by. She found herself longing for his return no matter how much she denied it and hid in her burrow, praying for sleep to eat up the hours as it had before.

Ashamed of herself, she tried to hide her relief when Shepherd came through the door, did her best not to look at him too long. It didn't make any difference. He knew that very first time, and it showed in the intensity of his curious expression when he smelled the air in her direction. He responded to it with a smile that crinkled the skin at the corners of his eyes, and by immediately taking her body with a practiced, calculating sensuality, watching her obsessively with those all-seeing eyes. It was as if he knew what was warring inside her, knew that she was losing—grasped that Claire found it harder to hate him, and struggled even to hate herself.

When she fell to pieces and the shame knifed into her, she began to cry as if lost. Shepherd played his hand, behaving seemingly patient, and continued the manipulative assault on her convictions by comforting her with deep purrs even as he mounted her, fucking the Omega until she forgot she had been upset in the first place.

The culmination of her ruin was the perpetual attack that persisted even in her sleep. Claire's dreams were filled with soft things, warmth, and the scent of her mate... his voice, the feel of his roughened hands slipping over her skin. The dream grew stronger nightly, and to her horror, she awoke half aware and throbbing for him to fill her. She instinctively reached for him the third or fourth time she'd awoken in that state, trailing her hand down his muscular body, pressing closer in her dazed need while she hummed in the dark. Shepherd responded with absolute enthusiasm, rolling his silken weight on top of her and groaning long and deep to find her already dripping wet. In that dreamlike mating, Claire could not get enough of his skin, cried out for him when his cock replaced where his fingers had been exploring, and held him as if he were hers, as if he were precious. When a corner of her mind rebelled, she shut it off, unwilling in that moment to recognize her failing, needing the fantasy just once where she was happy. And just like that, she lost another part of herself to a monster.

As he moved inside her, the thread resonating in joy, she realized how easy it could be—how dreamlike, how intoxicating—if she would only forget and submit. When she urged him to go faster, to give her more than slow, soothing thrusts, she came apart underneath him as he pounded away, the bond throbbing as powerfully as her pussy when she burst apart. Shepherd knotted deep, the sounds he created, the transcendent quality of his iron eyes, making it clear it was the most fulfilling orgasm he'd ever known.

He praised her for hours afterward, stroking and purring, and she wished he would not speak.

Claire did not want to hear how well she had pleased him or how beautiful he found her. It was making her remember that she was Claire and he was Shepherd, and all the things he had done, and all the ways she had failed in so short a time.

When she woke again, he was working at his desk, breathing in and out in a rhythmic purr that seemed so commonplace she hardly noticed it anymore. With him shirtless, Claire could see every line of his muscles, the dips and curves of a man built to break things. All that strength covered in a testament of murder...

Pulling a dress over her head, she sat at the edge of the bed and watched him.

Shepherd turned and looked at her, approval obvious between his lashes.

How far she'd fallen. Mortification made breath difficult. "How are the Omegas?"

The change in her captor was immediate. All trace of amusement vanished, and in its place was the hardness and dominance he exercised expertly. "They are exactly as they should be."

"Subjugated and imprisoned?" Claire challenged, standing up to force herself to pace. She should have been pacing for days... why had she stopped pacing? Why had she not asked sooner? What the fuck was wrong with her?

"Come here."

Her barked answer was immediate. "No."

She needed to go back to the status quo, to remembering to hate the father of her baby, not to admire his body... never to allow pleasant feelings for him. She should be wishing him dead, not prizing his attention. Wringing her hands, she marched, pointedly ignoring the giant rising from his chair to subdue her.

A meaty hand locked on her shoulder atop the claiming marks Shepherd had inflicted and tended each day. The discomfort of compressing tender flesh made Claire wince. She pressed her lips into a line and refused to look. Heat rose from his body, seeped into hers, and the smell—the necessary scent—forced her to close her eyes and focus to maintain defiance against a man who was her foe, not her lover.

"You will cease this at once." His voice was not hard.

"I will not."

His tone dropped considerably, it promised things. "Little one..."

Trying to shrug out of his grasp only enticed Shepherd's anger.

That was good, wasn't it? He had been too gentle, pretending he was not a beast who imprisoned and poisoned her. She needed to see the dragon, to hear the angry growls, to feel the thread buzz badly out of tune.

The fan of black lashes lifted, she looked him dead in the eye. "I will not stop."

"Your fear of change and this acting out is beneath you."

189

Frustrated, Claire clenched her fists. She wheezed.

A voice dripping reason came from lips that had tasted every inch of her skin. "If you wish to mate, you do not need to pick a fight to justify your desire to yourself. That is what you are doing, little one, expecting that my reaction will be to respond by mounting you—because you do not want to acknowledge that you are already wet and ready."

That was not what she was doing! Was it? A look of horror came to her face when she realized that she did smell of slick, that she was incredibly aroused... but she was also angry. She put her head in her hands, to hide her face, wishing she could just explode. "You do not understand me at all!"

"Then tell me what the point of this tantrum is?" he challenged in a mellow voice, still refusing to show the anger she wanted so badly to foster. "There will be no change to the Omega situation. You know that. I know that. Conversation on the topic is pointless and basely inflammatory... you desire my reaction, and we both know what you want me to do."

Claire started yanking on her hair.

Shepherd spoke again, "If you do not ask in this instance, then I will not give you what you want."

A sly smile, a nasty hateful grin, came to Claire's lips. She lowered her hands and looked into the unaffected silver. "I can tell you what I want! I want the Omegas to be treated as humans, not livestock. I want them to have the choice in whom they mate—to be safe and fed, and not treated like sex toys for your disgusting Followers!"

190

He still sounded so calm, but the embers were igniting. "I caution you to carefully consider your next words."

Her eyes fell to the expanse of his chest, staring hard where the thread was attached. She thought of the needle he'd jammed into her. She thought of his promise on the roof. "I am starting to remember myself. I will find a way to be free."

In one quick yank, he shook her roughly. "You will never leave this room!"

The customary discord was back, a shrill piercing pluck at the cord. Claire breathed in relief to feel it as Shepherd yanked her towards the bed. She was thrown down, the giant looming tall over her. But he did not touch her, only glared, his chest heaving, as if he wished to rip off her head. Then he turned and left, locking the door loudly to make his point.

Her victory was short-lived when uncomfortable loneliness set in. He did not return to her. At length, the blue-eyed Beta brought her next meal and Claire understood she had been upgraded to solitary confinement.

She was pregnant, her scent no longer enticing to his men. Shepherd could avoid her as much as he wished and have his peons bring her food... and she would simply have to endure it.

As she ate a dinner of lamb and roasted potatoes, she began to cry, missing Shepherd's presence and hating herself for it.

Chapter 11

It took a bit of creative thinking to learn the location of Claire's domicile before the occupation. All network systems in the Dome had been terminated, even COM towers were destroyed to ensure the population had little means to communicate or muster outside of face-to-face contact. All that was left was emergency hardware.

Shepherd's manipulation of the information and communication networks was practically complete, but not total.

There were still databases, servers filled with the information of the residents on each level—that was what Corday needed to access. Most of the Enforcer offices were currently occupied by Shepherd's Followers. Corday had scouted dozens. The few locations he'd found abandoned were in very hostile regions, the sectors' inner workings picked clean or totally demolished. But after two weeks of dangerous reconnaissance, he got lucky.

In the burned-out husk of a small, mid-level Enforcer station, Corday discovered one minuscule directory office untouched by the riots. The COMscreen functioned and, by some fucking miracle, booted when plugged into a battery.

Working quickly before anyone passing might notice his presence, Corday collected the former address of one Claire O'Donnell. Wasting no time, he shut off the valuable resource, tore out the memory cube, and climbed down seven levels to brave the cold neighborhood Claire had called her own.

The Omega had lived too near the slums for her home to ever have been considered safe. Everything was poorly maintained, sandwiched tightly, and painted in a faded wash of color. Her apartment had been ransacked, of course. Windows were shattered, knickknacks destroyed and anything of value gone. What remained was shoddy furniture and walls of expensive paper books.

In all the things taken, few books had been stolen.

The novels she adored had spines distorted by frequent use. Smirking, Corday found her favorites almost cliché, his lip twitching when a dog-eared copy of a pre-Dome romance was in a position of prominence. With careful fingers, he pulled it out and looked at the worn cover.

It was creased, it smelled like soapy vanilla. Returning it, Corday moved into the small space's only bedroom.

Everything was in the shade of robin's egg blue, styled in the simplistic, comfortable atmosphere Omegas required. The bedding still smelled of her, though it looked as if one of the rioters had rolled about in the linen. Taking a seat on the narrow mattress, Corday picked up the family photograph from her bedside table—her parents and Claire when she was just a girl. An Alpha father's hands rested on his little girl's shoulders. Beside them was a woman with a tight smile, a forced expression that tried to convey joy below surrendered eyes.

193

Claire was the image of her father, the same distinctive looks, the same black hair, but she had her mother's small frame and swanlike quality. She appeared fragile, but Corday knew she was stronger than she seemed.

Setting the photograph back, Corday began to poke through her collection of worthless jewelry even the looters had passed up. Under the lining of the small velvet box, he felt the outline of a ring and pulled back the fabric to find a worn gold band.

It was a wedding band. The same one worn by her mother in the photograph.

Without thought, Corday took it so he might return it to Claire. Because he was going to see her again. His Omega friend was sneaky and smart. She would find her way. Claire would not end up like the glassy-eyed Omegas the Enforcers had set free, the ones begging for some Alpha to claim them and give them a sense of purpose and relief. No... Claire was different.

She had to be.

***

Claire was unsure how many days had passed, what the hour was, how long she'd slept, or why she was always exhausted when she woke. Shepherd had not returned once since their fight.

There was no one to talk to, no soothing scent. There was nothing to do but obsess about the room and try not to think about how very lonely she was.

She cleaned every surface, going so far as to pull everything out of the dresser and refold each item with sharp corners. Even forcing distraction, more than once, she unwittingly allowed her thoughts to circle on the Alpha, tempting her to recall his more pleasing points.

The root of the issue was palpable. Claire wanted him back—his soothing purr, the heat of his body in her nest. Life was muddled by enforced seclusion, off-putting and confusing.

After shutting the last drawer, ready to move on to the bookshelf—what Shepherd had called her window—Claire turned and squeaked. A woman was standing behind her, so close they could have been touching.

Green eyes wide at seeing a stranger, Claire stammered, "Hello," wondering for a moment if she had lost her mind and begun hallucinating.

A smile, the lovely, polished, practiced grin of nobility, spread across pink lips. "Hello, pretty."

Claire could smell that the female was not what she seemed. The exotic beauty was an Alpha, but so delicate that the brunette could almost pass for Omega. Backing away, Claire found blue eyes tracking her movement and a small, amused smirk on those lips. "Who are you?"

The coolness of the woman's fingers made Claire instantly pull her head back. It did not stop the smirking woman from tracing her nail over the delicate skin under Claire's jaw. "I am Shepherd's beloved."

That string in her chest, the chain, writhed at those words. Pressing a hand defensively over her belly, Claire choked out, "I am Claire."

"Claire," a wealthy, accented voice drew out the pronunciation of the name.

A glint was in those oval eyes, something unwelcome and treacherous. The Alpha was dangerous, looking at her like a piece of meat, countering each step Claire took backwards until the Omega found herself trapped against the bed.

The intruder purred, "Be still, Omega."

Claire's voice dropped, her shoulders grew stiffer, and she said it again, "My name is Claire."

Pain burst across Claire's face. Pressing her hand to her bleeding lip, she stared in shock at the stranger who'd struck her.

"You're drenched in him." The Alpha female sniffed. "Lie on the bed and spread your legs so I may see."

"I don't know who the fuck you are, but back off!"

There was a tutting sound in the air. "You can obey, or I will have Shepherd force you."

"Then get him to force me... I don't spread just because an Alpha bitch commands it."

Before she might escape, an unyielding hand circled Claire's throat. She was forced back until her knees bent and the Omega's back hit the mattress. Clawing at the grip crushing her windpipe, Claire stared up into the unblinking blue eyes of a killer—what she saw there inspired more fear than she'd ever known.

The woman's hand stroked under Claire's skirt, fingers jamming inside her to swirl painfully around her dry womb. The brunette drew them out and tasted. "You are pregnant. How interesting."

A second hand came to grip Claire's neck. A tighter squeeze and her world began to go dark.

"Svana." It was one word, spoken in a very dangerous tone.

The brunette cocked her head at the man standing in the door.

"My love." Svana smiled. "Your plaything's eyes are the wrong color. My eyes are blue."

"Release the Omega's throat."

With a playful smirk and a quick flourish of her fingers, Svana let Claire go. Coughing, sucking in air, Claire scrambled back, wide eyes looking at Shepherd, looking at the man who, though bonded to her, stood by and did nothing. Everything was wrong, the cord was jangled, and with horror, Claire witnessed total love in the expression Shepherd offered the Alpha female approaching him.

The exotic beauty petted her mate's chest. Svana purred, "I have missed you. Get rid of your toy. I only have a few hours before I must return."

197

Cupping the woman's face, Shepherd explained, "The Omega is not permitted to leave this room."

Svana shrugged her shoulders. "Then she can join in or watch. What a pity I missed her last cycle. We have not shared a heated Omega in some time."

Shallow pants, that was all Claire could manage as she pressed herself against the wall and realized how truly depraved the man who had hooked an anchor into her chest really was. Now she understood. No chemicals from pregnancy, no pair-bond could change it. She was nothing to Shepherd. She had been manipulated to care for a monster who loved another—to be what the female had insisted: his plaything.

"Claire, you will go into the bathroom and remain until I come for you."

He had spoken her name. Dumbstruck, Claire stared at the two of them, stared as Shepherd—as her mate—touched another female affectionately.

When she made no movement to follow the command, a furious head snapped up and his silver eyes narrowed menacingly. "Go."

She obeyed. Each step felt like walking on glass, but the pain was a blessing, a gift from the goddess of the Omegas. Claire's mind began to clear, the influence of the cord began to weaken, and she began to feel nothing at all.

She closed the door behind her and sat alone. Staring the future dead in the face, she knew just what hell looked like.

The sound of the two Alphas fucking was nothing. Breathing was nothing. Where she had been slowly settling into life in that little grey room, she was now free of such petty things as further existence. A great crack ran through her chest, a fissure that bled vile, noxious gas into the air while Claire sat there in the dark, the music of evil coming through the door. There was nothing left for the greasy thread to hold onto. There was nothing left inside her... but she was still horribly Claire.

Later, Shepherd woke her where she slept against the wall. He pulled her up and sat her on the lid of the toilet so he could press a wet towel to her split lip. She looked him dead in the eye, a fierce, penetrating, nightmare of a gaze. When he said nothing, she began to laugh at him, loudly, the noise saturated in judgment.

He was pathetic... disgusting. And he was dead to her.

The expression that came was one of confusion—the look a small boy cornered by bullies wears. It was perfect.

A hard voice growled, "Svana is dangerous."

Claire only laughed harder, the hoarse sound ruined by the damage to her throat. She laughed until her face was red, until her insides hurt. She laughed until she had to push past Shepherd and puke in the sink. Standing straight, she wiped her stinging mouth with the back of her hand and, still snickering, walked out of the bathroom and into a room that, if she had any reason to breathe, would have smelled utterly tainted.

It was just four grey walls, every crack known to her—a box with nothing in it.

Her nest was a wreck, so Claire lay down in the middle of the floor and closed her eyes. It almost felt like she was merging with the earth, becoming one with the endless, lifeless room.

It was beautiful.

When she woke, it was bright outside, Claire felt it in her bones. She stared at the ceiling imagining the way sunlight must glint off the Dome. She was alone again. Food was on the table waiting for her. Standing, she took the plate, carried it to the bathroom, and flushed everything down the toilet. Dropping the vitamin, her lips sounded out the word, "plop," as it fell into the swishing water. The empty plate was returned to the tray and she went right back to her warm outline on the floor. A whole day passed.

The door opened. Her listless eyes found the blue-eyed Beta had come with another tray. The Follower moved past her as if she did not exist.

Devoid of feeling, Claire croaked, "I don't know your name."

Deadpan, he answered, "I'm Jules. Shepherd desires that you do not forget the vitamin."

The empty tray was taken. He walked by without even looking at her.

The door was locked and Claire made sure she followed Shepherd's mandate. She flushed all the food, and unquestionably, did not forget the vitamin. After all, now that she was hollow inside, it was nice to have the grey room to herself. She showered, changed her clothing, brushed her hair... all the things living people were supposed to do. Then she went right back to that spot on the floor to rot.

Inevitably, enough time passed. The sound of combat boots thudded against the ground and the devil was crouching over her. A purr sounded and Claire opened her eyes, entirely unimpressed.

She felt nothing.

Shepherd picked her up, her body hanging limp, and took off the fresh dress, putting her in the bed. The sheets must have been changed. Either that or she had lost the pattern of Shepherd's scent. Everything just smelled flat. The man slid in beside her, naked, and eased up close. As he did everything he wanted, taking what she never offered, he pressed his chest to hers and growled.

Nothing.

He spread her legs, growled again, and let his fingers dance between her thighs. Whatever he was doing, Claire only stared at the ceiling, seeing instead the overcast night sky. She did not make a noise when a foreign presence pushed uncomfortably into her unprepared body. She just lay there through all of it, unsure how long he tried, how hard he worked... because she didn't care. An odd stretch let her know that the sweating, grunting thing had knotted.

Still nothing.

While their bodies were locked, she heard the distant sound of a low, raspy voice and ignored it. There were tugs at her hair, the smooth strokes of hands. Claire yawned. Sleep was immediate.

Walking through the Undercroft where her kind had been locked away, Nona maintained her ramrod spine despite the two large Followers yanking her about. She had not been troubled or questioned for weeks, and wondered what asinine things they would waste her time with now. When the door opened and she was pressed into the room, even she could not hide the quirk in her brow or the sudden feeling of dread when she found it was not the Beta, Jules, who sat at the table.

Even seated, the Alpha was massive.

"She seems to think standing as you do serves a purpose as well. But you are still Omega and you know that resistance to one such as I is pointless," Shepherd explained, his voice conversational, though the nature of his expression was anything but pleasant.

Nona took a seat without being asked, old enough to know better than to engage male taunts.

The man began. "You are the de facto leader of this Omega pack—"

Nona interjected, "I am not. We function as a democracy."

"How have you found the provided accommodations?"

"Prison-like," Nona answered, watching him just as callously as he watched her.

Shepherd was not impressed with her bravado. "I have supplied you with clean water, wholesome food, warm blankets, shelter..."

"Your rationalization is faulty." Nona tapped the desk. "All those comforts are only to prepare the Omegas for slavery to a stranger."

"You are the one who corrupted her into thinking the way she does."

Now that was interesting. Cocking her head, Nona asked, "Excuse me?"

"Of the eight Omegas pair-bonded since arrival into my keeping, all have accepted their place—behaving as they should."

It was foolish to smile, one good swing and he could rip her head off her shoulders, but Nona allowed the expression. There was a catch to his statement, an underlying irritation that exposed his own less than perfect relationship. "There is nothing I can tell you that would make Claire be what she is not. I have droned on for hours about the foods I know she likes, her hobbies... all questions you could have asked her yourself."

"Your only use to me, old woman, is information that will help settle my mate." Contemplating how easily he could crush the old woman's throat, Shepherd warned, "Do not think to posture or advise."

"Then get to the point."

The slight flaring of his silver eyes, the sudden stink of hostility—he was far less steady in his aloofness than he pretended. "I am beginning to

203

suspect you have outlived your usefulness. There is room for your body to swing next to the other Omegas."

"If there is something wrong with Claire, I would do anything to help her," Nona argued, more than happy to honestly express her anger. "Whatever insight you seek, just ask."

"My mate has grown withdrawn."

Scowling, Nona wondered how the hell he could possibly be surprised. With her lips in a line, she waited for the man to continue.

Shepherd leaned nearer, barking, "Are you going to say nothing?"

"I am unsure what you expect me to say," Nona maintained. "That is not a word I have ever heard used to describe Claire. She is usually quite vocal. Whatever she is now, you have created in your treatment of her."

"At the separate deaths of her parents, what drew her out of her melancholy?"

"Time, and the support of people she loved."

It was clear the answer was unacceptable, that the giant had reached the end of his patience.

The man made her sick and the sentiment was obvious in Nona's accusation. "Do you behave this way with her, as well? She won't respond to it."

"I am very careful with Claire."

Something in his words made her feel he was lying, or that he was careful in the way one holds a newborn kitten—an unnatural way to behave with a mate. Sniffing the air, leaning forward to make her appraisal obvious, Nona found very little of Claire's scent on the man. "And you have studied her like a specimen, with information gathered from outside sources. Why? To manipulate the situation to your liking?"

"Of course."

"Apparently your strategy has failed." That was it. "There is nothing I can say to help you, Alpha."

Shepherd's glare threatened torment. "There will be no food for any Omega over the next three days. All will be notified that you were the cause of starvation."

**

How funny the world was. Everything was in reverse. Claire sat in a chair, her head resting atop her palm, while Shepherd was the one pacing. Back and forth, back and forth. He was like an agitated dinosaur.

Claire made a noise.

The great hulk stopped and looked at her. He spoke.

She heard nothing.

Her thin fingers began to drum against the table. And again the beast prowled. Eventually, he tugged her up, as he had done with every visit, and he took her dress. It was the same: the mattress at her back, his useless growl, and then whatever tricks he had thought up to seduce her body. Shepherd thought to be clever, smoothing a great portion of lubricant on his jutting cock before he began the rut. He thrust this way and that way, just like his disturbed pacing. He tried everything to get a response, even trying to coax a kiss from her slack lips, to whisper in her ear, to caress and stare into eyes that were far away.

"Little one, come back."

She would never come back. Not to him. Not to the beast who had made her want him once and betrayed her so thoroughly.

Claire fell asleep while Shepherd was still moving inside her.

Eventually, the Alpha figured out what she was doing with the meals delivered while he was away. Not that it was hard to discover when she did not even look at the food he brought her. His mate was growing wan, dark circles under her eyes, and no matter what he pushed between her lips, she would not swallow. She would only stare with those dead eyes, stare straight at him, daring him to try and make her eat.

As he slammed his hand on the table, the metal groaned. Claire stared right back, and lazily spat out everything in her mouth, letting it fall into her lap. There was a roar, the entirety of her tray thrown across the room to slam against the wall. A paw wrenched her from the chair, a blanket wrapped too tight around her. Shepherd had her in his arms.

The metal was thrown back, her concrete walls disappeared. They passed a fire extinguisher she had seen before, a blue door, a room full of COMmonitors, only that time there were men in the room, men in the halls—Followers saluting the giant who ignored them as he stormed past.

The sound of boots on concrete stairs, grunted orders Claire ignored, and a door opened to blasting cold. Atmosphere, fresh air... she'd seen such things lying on the floor staring through the ceiling. It was nothing special. Claire closed her eyes.

Shepherd was having none of it. Great arms shook her, jarring her body until her eyes opened. He set her down on her feet and backed away so that she had to stand on her own. Claire did, knowing something that no other man on that terrace knew. A mind could learn entirely new things almost instantly when it was utterly devoid, eyes saw minutiae that thinking minds missed. She stood on her own two feet and looked up at the snowing sky... feeling the large white flakes melt on her cheeks.

Snow that thick was a sign the Dome had been damaged, the arctic creeping in. The engineers responsible for colonial safety had failed.

Hadn't they all failed?

Seeing her stand, the beast drew a relieved breath behind her.

No one could have known what she was going to do. Not one of them could have suspected it. Under the pretense of a yawn, Claire cracked her neck, and rolled her shoulders in a way that loosened the blanket. Then, in a burst of speed, she darted like a hare and bounded over the edge of the Citadel terrace to fall into darkness before any could reach her.

The inertia of limp bodies absorbed force far differently than stiff flailing ones. Claire knew that. What she didn't know was that even high fluffy piles of snow really, really hurt when you jumped off a building to land in one.

There was a general outcry above her, but the fresh powder sucked her in, hiding her long enough to slip down an icy corridor only someone as small as an Omega could fit through. Then she did what she did best. Claire ran.

From above, it looked as if she had simply vanished. Since she was already dead inside, she may as well have.

Thank you for reading Born to be Bound.
Shephard and Claire's story is far from over.
Read BORN TO BE BROKEN now!

Craving more? Omegaverse Dark Romance at its most gut-wrenching! Jealous, possessive, and willing to commit any sin to steal his mate, Shepherd is the antihero book boyfriend you've been waiting for.

•Born to be Bound — Violent, calculating, and incapable of remorse, Shepherd demands his new mate's adoration. Her attention. Her body.

•Born to be Broken — He doesn't know how to love his captive Omega. But Shepherd is determined to learn.

•Reborn — the nature of their pair-bond has consumed Claire to the point that she has difficulty differentiating where her feelings begin and Shepherd's machinations end.

•Stolen —He took her with violence while none intervened. He broke her, swearing he'd put her back together.

The Wren's Song Series is a dark, sinister Omegaverse Reverse Harem tale for those with twisted tastes and a love for complete power exchange.

•Branded Captive — Wren can't sing like a bird. She can't speak at all. The Alpha kingpin and his pack didn't buy the Omega to hear it talk.

•Silent Captive — Wren is caught in the clutches of three dangerous Alphas, each with their own selfish designs.

•Broken Captive — Caspian has marked her, Toby has claimed her, and Kieran is unwillingly caught in her spell.

•Ravaged Captive — Drenched in wealth and power, Caspian holds my city by the throat. No man or woman denies him, not even me.

Carnal, filthy, and unbelievably satisfying. My bestselling Omegaverse Dark Romance awaits those daring enough to take a taste.

•The Golden Line — They call me brutal. They call me unrepentant. They call me possessive. I am all these things and much, much worse.

Like your men in doting, affectionate, and utterly possessive? Read my Reverse Harem Dark Romance. The Irdesi Empire Series is smoldering page-turner sure to satisfy.

•Sigil — He will have her. Even if he must crush empires. Even if he must harm her for her own good. Even if he must share her with his brothers. Sigil will be his.

•Sovereign — Sovereign tends his reluctant consort. His many Brothers lavish her with attention, each exercising their own brand of seduction to woo their species' only female.

If your tastes run to brooding alpha males, my hit dark romance, this Regency Dark Romance will scratch your itch.

•Dark Side of the Sun — Greedy, cunning, cruel, Gregory claims to love her, offers to kill for her... but lies come easily to his tongue.

Obsession and the most twisted "love" fill this smoldering page-turner. Beware, the dark horror ahead.

•Catacombs — The vampire king has found his queen, locking her away for his own sick pleasures.

Taboo horror that will worm its way into your darker thoughts and keep you up all night? Whatever you do, don't follow the white rabbit!

•The White Queen — The devil owes the Hatter a favor... and he knows just what he wants for his prize.

•Immaculate — But my knees have been sullied in worship to a vacant altar. Everything I was taught is a lie. There is no God here.

Love good, old fashioned desire? Take a turn with this prohibition era romance.

•A Taste of Shine — Something isn't right about the new girl in town. Charlotte Elliot swears, she drinks, and she's trying too damn hard to fit in with the simple folk.

•A Shot in the Dark — Matthew is determined to find his run-away sweetheart. And then he's going to marry her.

Join my Facebook group, Addison Cain's Dark Longing's Lounge, for sneak peeks, free loot, and a whole lot of fun! Ask me anything! I'd love to chat with you.

Now, please enjoy an extended excerpt of BORN TO BE BROKEN...

BORN TO BE BROKEN

Alpha's Claim, Book Two

Chapter 1

By the time she'd found his home, Claire could little more than crawl. Scratching at the portal, fingers numb, she slumped to the floor. When the door cracked and squinting eyes showed in the dark, had she the capacity, Claire would have laughed. Never had a man looked more shocked.

She was filthy; stringy hair wet from snow and sweat, limbs badly scraped from her fall. About her throat, a bruise tellingly shaped in a handprint circled like a sad necklace. That was nothing compared to the state of her feet when he tried to help her stand. Torn and bleeding, more skin had been worn away than was sound. Corday hoisted her from the ground, her freezing body flush to his, and locked the door.

"Claire!" He vigorously rubbed his hands up and down the trembling woman's back. "I have you."

It's a good thing he did; once the door locked her eyes rolled back in her skull, Claire unconscious. Corday rushed her to his shower, cranked on the heat, and stood with her under the spray. Her lips were blue, and no wonder considering that temperatures on this level of the Dome had grown near freezing. The Beta stripped off her ruined dress and washed every rivulet of blood from his friend, finding more bruises, more wounds, more reasons to hate Shepherd.

213

The gauze at her shoulder he'd left for last, grateful at least something had been tended to. But as it grew saturated, he grew worried by what was hinted at under the bandage. Peeling it back, Corday cursed to see what the beast had done to her. Shepherd's claiming marks, the tissue red and distorted—even after what looked like weeks of healing, her shoulder was a fucking mess.

The monster had mutilated her.

The water turned as cold as Corday's blood. He pulled her out, dried her the best he could, and tucked Claire into the warmth of his bed. There she lay, naked and badly damaged, a little color coming back to her hollowed cheeks. One at a time, he uncovered limbs, tending scrapes, bandaging wounds, doing his best to preserve her modesty. That didn't mean he didn't see them, the telling bruises mottling her inner thighs.

She looked almost as bad as the Omegas the resistance had rescued…

It frightened him. Not one of those women was thriving. Even safe, they deteriorated—hardly spoke, hardly ate. More of them had died, and though the Enforcers could not pinpoint the cause, Brigadier Dane was certain with all that they'd suffered—the children and mates that had been taken from them—they had simply lost the will to live.

Claire had to be different.

Left arm, right arm, both elbows sluggishly bled. Salve and bandages were the best Corday could offer. But there was nothing he could do for her throat; the mottled yellow-brown bruises were not fresh. The Omega's injuries grew far more complicated with her legs—both kneecaps were grotesque; one gash deep enough to require stitches. He did his best with butterfly sutures, closing the gap of torn flesh, lining up the skin so that it might stand a chance of mending. Her joints would swell—that was unavoidable—and he hesitated to ice them as she was already shivering and still cold to the touch.

"You're gonna be okay, Claire," he promised. "You're safe with me."

Claire opened bloodshot eyes; she looked at the Beta whose face she could read like a book. He was scared for her. "It doesn't hurt."

"Shhh." He leaned down, smiling to see her awake. Stroking the wet, tangled hair from her face, he said, "Rest your throat."

She complied, and Corday worked quickly to finish, disinfecting every abrasion on her outer thighs, knees, and shins. Her feet were a different matter. There was little he could do, and she would hardly be able to walk in the days to come. He picked out the detritus, noting how she didn't move or twitch even when a fresh wave of blood followed a large chunk of glass once it was pulled free. He wrapped her feet tight, and said a prayer to all three Gods that the open wounds would not fester.

Once it looked like she was asleep, he rose.

Claire's hand shot out, her bruised fingers clawing into his sleeve. "Don't go!"

"You need medicine," Corday soothed, weaving his fingers with hers.

Claire held tighter, disjointed and afraid. "Don't leave me alone."

Brushing a pile of bandage wrappers to the floor, Corday did as she wished. He slipped under the covers beside her, offering body heat and a safe place to rest. Claire let him hold her, laying her head on his shoulder, still.

Ashamed to ask, beyond pathetic, she whispered, "Will you purr for me?"

Such a thing was an act of intimacy between lovers and family, but there was no hesitation in the Beta. Corday pulled in a deep breath and started the rumbling vibration at once. The sound was a little off—the act being something he was unaccustomed to—and though it lacked the richness of an Alpha purr, it was infinitely comforting in that moment.

"That's nice." Exhausted, Claire sighed. "Please don't stop."

Corday thumbed a spilling tear from her cheek. "I won't, Claire."

In the voice of a broken thing, Claire began to feel more than endless choking malaise; she felt disgust... for herself. "I hate that name."

* * *

Huddled close to her friend, like children whispering secrets, Claire woke. Though her body ached, she was warm, surrounded in a scent of safety, and grateful for the boyish smile Corday offered once she'd pried her sticky lashes apart.

Cautious and gentle, he smoothed her tangled hair. "You look much better."

They were so close she could see the night's stubble on his cheek, smell his breath.

He seemed so real.

Sucking her split lower lip into her mouth, Claire felt the sting. Tasting the scab left when that woman, Svana, had struck her for refusing to spread, made the nightmare real again. It was as if Svana were in the room with her, as if the Alpha's hands remained wrapped around her throat.

Claire struggled to breathe.

Corday broke through her growing terror. "You're okay, Claire. I'll keep you safe."

It wasn't a dream, it was real. Claire grew to understand that the more Corday spoke, the more he touched her, the more she felt the sun on her face.

How had she even come to be there?

She *was* separated from Shepherd, in a great deal of physical discomfort, naked, and Corday had taken her in, despite the fact that she had drugged him—lied to him.

She had to remind herself out loud; she had to make herself remember. "I jumped off the back terrace of the Citadel… crashed into snow."

"And you ran here," Corday finished for her.

She had, before air had even returned to her lungs she'd scampered up and fled. "I ran as fast as I could... right to your door." Voice breaking, trembling something fierce, Claire sobbed, "I'm sorry, Corday."

Seeing her panic, he tried to calm her. "There is nothing to be sorry for."

"I drugged you," she whispered. "I lied. And now he'll find you. He'll hurt you."

"He won't." Corday grew earnest and severe. "You can trust me. There is no need for you to lie to me again. I can't help you if you lie."

"If I had taken you to the Omegas, he would have killed you, just as he killed Lilian and the others." Claire looked to the pillowcase lightly crusted with her blood. "He punished me... I'm pregnant."

Corday already knew. He'd smelled it almost the instant Claire had been in his arms. There was only one way such a thing could have come to pass. Shepherd had forced another heat cycle.

There was very little he could say, little he could do, but one thing Corday could offer her. He looked her dead in the eye and asked, "Do you want to remain that way?"

What a question... Claire had to think, recognized she had been clinging to the Beta to the point where it must have made his shoulder ache. Easing her hold, she measured the little bit of human that she still was, and knew she had not wanted a baby yet. More so, she had foolishly allowed herself to develop an attachment to the monster who had filled her womb, a monster who was using her like a broodmare—a beast whose lover had tried to kill her.

Claire pressed her hand to the tiny life growing inside her. She could rid herself of the issue; abortion was a common practice, probably accessible even now. She could have Shepherd carved out of her.

After a shuddering breath she admitted her horrific truth, "I don't feel anything, you know. Inside… I feel nothing at all."

He gave her space, offering a lopsided smile. "I know it might seem like the world has ended for you, Claire, but you are free now. You're a survivor."

She could not help but sadly smile at a man who would never understand. "Survivor? What kind of future do you see for me? I was pair-bonded to a monster to be his toy, drugged into an unnatural heat cycle, impregnated against my will so I would grow devoted, and then forced to listen to the Alpha who was supposed to be my mate fuck his lover—a very scary Alpha female who wrapped her hands around my throat, who shoved her fingers inside me right in front of him."

He couldn't stop a grimace. "Shhh. This can be made right."

"It's okay for us both to admit there isn't going to be a happy ending for me." Claire sat up, holding the sheet to her chest, empty. "I have no future, but I can still fight for them."

Brushing back her hair, wanting to pull her nearer, Corday restrained the desire to embrace the sad-eyed woman. "If you step outside that door and try to take on Shepherd, you won't win."

"I won't win... but I *am* going to act out." A goal, something to cling to, hardened her voice. Claire sneered. "I'm going to do everything I can to make noise. And if they catch me, I'll make sure they kill me."

"Please listen to me," Corday grew urgent, afraid to scare her off should he say the wrong thing. "Let's talk this through. The best thing you can do right now is grow stronger. "

"I intend to." She nodded, knowing he misunderstood. "Shepherd once told me there is no good in the people of Thólos. He was wrong. This occupation has stripped away our pretenses; it has made us naked to our nature. Don't you see? Integrity, kindness—it exists here..." Claire closed her eyes, nestled nearer once again. "You, Corday, are a good man."

He didn't hesitate to pull her flush. "And you're a good woman."

Resting her cheek on his shoulder, she sighed. She might have been a *good woman* once, but the truth was, she was not a person anymore. She was a shadow.

"I want you to know that while you were gone, we uncovered the distributors of the counterfeit heat-suppressants. Omegas were rescued. They are recovering and protected. The drugs were destroyed; every last man paid for his crimes."

There was a flutter in Claire's chest, a moment of feeling she tore to pieces before it might infect her. "Thank you, Corday."

"You are a part of that, you know?" Boyish eagerness, a desire to see Claire pleased, infected his grin. "Your determination—you fought for them. They have you to thank for their freedom."

"I didn't do anything but get raped and cry about it."

"You're wrong." Corday took her cheek, made her meet his eye. "You stood up to the biggest monster of them all. You have escaped him twice now. *You* are strong, Claire."

But she wasn't. "No... you don't understand. The pair-bond, the pregnancy... I started to care for him, to need him." Saying it out loud made her mouth taste of vomit. "I was weak."

Corday knew none of that was her fault. "Given the circumstances, what happened was only natural."

"I don't know what it was... but *it* was. I stopped seeing a monster and wanted the attention of the man. And once he'd persuaded my affection, he made it the world's sickest joke. I should be grateful, I guess. Listening to him with her... it ripped the pair-bond out. He can't control me now."

The total lack of emotion in Claire's voice disturbed Corday. Whatever Shepherd had done had damaged the Omega, and a part of him wondered if every expression she was making was only because she was supposed to remember things like breathing and blinking.

Oblivious to the apprehension in her friend, Claire continued. "I get it now. This breach was not about gaining power. We're his puppets, falling rabid at the snap of his fingers. We dance on his stage. Shepherd, his Followers, they're punishing us all for…" she scoffed under her breath, "for blind ignorance. For allowing what was done to them."

"You are free of him, of his lies, and his evil, Claire. Remember that."

"The Dome is cracked. It's snowing outside. Not frost, *real snow*. We are not free of him, not when we let that happen. We let this all happen."

"We can take back Thólos."

Claire's breath hitched. "Not so long as he is alive."

* * *

"Your Omega escaped through a broken drainage gate. Blood on the scene shows the direction in which she fled and that her bearing was not affected by broken legs. The trail was lost when she slid below mid-level and moved out over accumulating sludge."

"How much blood?" Shepherd demanded, skimming the report in his hand for anything relevant.

"Considering the distance she fell, minimal. Internal bleeding may be an issue."

His unforgiving gunmetal glare caught the light. Impatient, Shepherd growled, "She has not eaten in almost a week. She will not have been able to manage a great distance malnourished, shoeless, and bleeding."

"Was she suffering from morning sickness?"

Shepherd turned toward his desk, his attention going back to the report. "Hunger strike."

Jules, unsurprised by such a statement, remained blank. "When she is returned, what are your expectations of Miss O'Donnell?"

Exceedingly irate, Shepherd hissed, "For her to resume her duty as my mate."

Only psychological damage would lead a pregnant, pair-bonded Omega to hunger strike and jump off a building in madness. Jules grew blunt. "And if that's not possible? Whom do you intend to serve as surrogate Alpha to see to her until she delivers your heir?"

Muscles straining, Shepherd warned, "You presume much, Jules. She will be returned and her behavior corrected."

Jules was second-in-command for a good reason—he was shrewd and willing to act. Employing candor, he stated, "Without physical contact the Omega will willingly accept, she may miscarry."

223

Shepherd was not to be gainsaid by man or woman. His final order was issued. "You are dismissed."

Grasping that the situation was beyond his original assessment, Jules saluted and removed himself from the room.

Shepherd took to his desk, alone. Memorizing the reports flashing on his COMscreen, every so often he habitually glanced behind him, expecting to see Claire pacing. But she was not there. She was gone... He knew in his bones that his mate had sought out the *noble* man who had offered help. The Beta would take her in, tend her, comfort her, touch her. The very idea another might hold her... act as a surrogate... infuriated him.

Gnashing his teeth, Shepherd swore. The Beta would die screaming.

Had Shepherd not purred, growled, stroked, followed every instinct to rouse her back from her stupor? He'd even tried to explain. *Him!* The Alpha, the strongest who was never questioned, had tried to reason with an Omega. But she had not even blinked.

She'd slipped so far out of his grasp.

It was her vocation to stay, to be devoted, to love him, to obey. Had he not seen to her needs? Had he not given her nice dresses and the best food? Had he not spent hours simply petting the girl until she was completely content? What was one unpleasant situation compared to that?

Had he not saved her life in more ways than one?

Impregnating her ensured her survival, justified her maintenance to his followers. No one could question the safekeeping of his baby. More importantly, it gave her purpose and distraction. Shepherd could not tell her in so many words—she was not one of them, remained far too determined in her ideal of *goodness* to comprehend the greatness of his calling. Furthermore, the reasoning behind his actions was unnecessary for her to know. Shepherd knew if Claire realized the true nature of what was coming, she would only fret more. She would cry for her pathetic citizens instead of giving all her attention to him. Direct treachery was best: it kept him in control of her fate. But she was willful, so damn obstinate with her foolish romantic notions.

Shepherd's fist crashed against the table. He roared, upended the entire thing until papers flew and his COMscreen cracked against the cold floor.

Svana's unexpected arrival had been infuriatingly problematic. Not only was she displeased by what she had found, Svana would have ripped Claire's beautiful eyes out had Shepherd not pacified his beloved once she'd seen what he'd kept hidden away. You don't reason with provoked Alphas, you show action. Had he not fucked her loudly, broadcasting his favor to ensure the territorial female did not view the Omega as a threat, Claire would have been murdered the first moment he left her alone. He had done what was necessary, for both of the women.

It was the price to keep Claire.

Yet he had lost her anyway, even before she had run. Watching her mentally slip away, his rush of anger, his outright fury... it was the same rage that had burned him when he rose from the Undercroft to murder Premier Callas... only to find the leader of Thólos—the man who'd sentenced his mother to the Undercroft—was richly laced with the scent of Svana's sex.

Shepherd had drawn a deep breath, momentarily stunned as he processed what could not be—until he understood what Svana had done.

The speech he'd prepared for his greatest enemy, the one perfected night after night caged underground, was forgotten. What should have been a quick death, the body to be displayed, ended in blood dripping from the ceiling, Premier Callas' entrails flung all over the floor.

And then came pain far more horrific than any agony his Da'rin markings might produce. His beloved had defiled herself, purposefully tainted her body by mating with the enemy.

Shepherd had confronted Svana, the woman he had loved from the first moment they'd met in the dark, the ethereal creature who was his whole life, who held his soul in her beautiful hands. The woman who had set him free, empowered him to gain control of the Undercroft—the very woman he'd killed for, suffered for, ached for.

Since their first sexual experience, Shepherd had only ever lain with the occasional estrous high Omega his beloved had procured for them—so they could fulfil the animal urge to rut together as they were meant to. For lesser beings, Alpha/Alpha pairings were difficult, as there was no pair-bond, and it was in their natures to challenge for dominance. But the two of them were beyond such sordid behavior. Or so he'd thought. He had never wavered... not once.

She had.

She had fucked the Premier, thrown what they had aside for some distorted ploy, as the final undiscussed crux in her plan. As Shepherd heard her speak on the matter, as she convincingly painted a grand scenario, he could not bring himself to question what she'd *never mentioned*. Svana had planned her seduction all along. Though she held Shepherd and spoke of her love, he was attuned to her; he could smell what was wrong in her scent. What had been done was even worse than he'd originally believed; Svana had chemically forced an unlikely ovulation. She wanted to bear the child of her enemy... to have a traitor's lineage continue the line—a man who wasn't infected with Da'rin, who was born with superior bloodlines—a man who might even be the carrier of the *alleged* antibody to the Red Consumption in his veins.

Not like Shepherd, who didn't know which of the countless prisoners who'd raped his mother had fathered him. His blood had not been fostered through generations with access to secret science and inoculations against disease. Instead, he was disfigured by Da'rin that burned in the sun and would always mark him as a castoff.

She had not voiced it, but Shepherd interpreted the truth. Svana found him wanting in the most primal of ways.

All those years, Shepherd's fidelity had been one sided. Svana did not hesitate to admit she'd taken other lovers. Hadn't he? After all, were they not Alphas? Was it not their right? She had stroked his chest and smiled so perfectly, reminding him that what they shared was beyond the physical. They shared a great destiny, an eternal spiritual bond of love.

Gutted, Shepherd had fulfilled his duty to his loyal Followers, to the dead mother he hardly remembered. Thólos fell, everyone playing their part to perfection; yet he was less for it. The world had shifted, he had achieved greatness, but what was he left with? Nothing. A big black hole where the light had gone out. He was incomplete.

But then he smelled something untainted hiding under the poignant stink of decay. Like a gift from the Gods, Claire was delivered; unlikely virtue born out of the filth of Thólos. A lotus. Claire, with her convictions and her timid bravery, walked up to a man like him—stubbornly waited for hours, a lamb amongst the wolves—to beg for help from the very villain inflicting suffering on the friends she would save.

One breath of her and he would have taken her, heat or no. The Gods had simplified his spiritual culmination by delivering her in estrous.

As he'd rutted the willful, strange thing, Shepherd found she wriggled so wonderfully, felt so perfectly snug encasing his cock, that he had to ensure she could never leave. As Svana had claimed their *devotion* was beyond the physical, their love divine, Shepherd felt perfectly justified in taking Claire, in creating a corporeal mate—an attachment that would only benefit the unruly Omega. He bonded to keep Claire for himself, his reward for service to the greater good of mankind reborn. The green-eyed little one's purity was now his own, her nearness succor. In Claire, Shepherd had regained that missing piece, the covetous need to possess something innocent, achieved.

Yet, now his bonded mate was gone with his child in her belly, wandering a city that was destined for plague.

The Omega would never come back to him willingly, not while the pair-bond was so damaged. Shepherd would have to return Claire by force.

He could almost hear the echo of her words in the air: *do not give me cause to hate you more.*

What had gone through the mind of the Omega he'd found unconscious on the bathroom floor? He'd anticipated anger, but found something impaired far beyond his reasoning. His coupling with Svana had left Claire unresponsive and empty—left the cord so fractured, all Shepherd could feel from her was an echo of desolation.

It was not a sensation he enjoyed.

No amount of attention or space had made a difference. Glassy eyes looked at him with judgment and hatred no matter how he tended her, touched her, or purred. All her favorite foods had been prepared, new dresses put in her drawer... she had not even noticed.

Claire O'Donnell belonged to him. Shepherd would find her, drag her back... and force feed her if he fucking had to. He would make her adore him like she was supposed to. Because she was his, only his, and he did not share his things. Ever.

He had even prevented the sharing of her body with his beloved. Was that not something?

* * *

Corday had rushed to carry out his mission for the resistance, eager to return to Claire. It wasn't because he didn't trust her to stay put, it was because he didn't trust her at all. The look in her eyes when Senator Kantor had arrived to guard her had been nothing but calculating. There was none of her former fear or skittishness, her reaction numbed as she sized up the Alpha.

The Senator could see the change in her as well, Kantor reacting with cautious courtesy. They exchanged pleasantries, Corday made them coffee, and then he left to meet Brigadier Dane. Corday's duties kept him out past dark, and the Enforcer was utterly unprepared for the sight that met his eyes when he returned home.

Claire was asleep, curled up on the couch next to Senator Kantor, who was boldly purring in the dark.

230

A stab of something unwelcome drew Corday to frown. "Did she ask you to do that?"

"No. I knew what would lull her to sleep," Senator Kantor answered in a hushed tone. "Rebecca struggled to fall asleep too. I learned a lot tending my wife in the years the Gods blessed me with my Omega."

It was taboo to speak of deceased mates. Corday was surprised to hear the Alpha mention Rebecca—especially considering the sad circumstances of her long ago murder by Kantor's political adversary. It had been a sensation and had led to Senator Bergie, several of his staff, and even Bergie's son being incarcerated in the Undercroft.

Unsure what to say in response, Corday lit a few candles, and dragged a seat over from the kitchen, his face grim as he looked at the sleeping girl. "How was she today?"

"Better once she ate—less catatonic, more cognizant." Senator Kantor studied the wasted thing. "Miss O'Donnell's physical reaction after having parted from the father will be complicated. The pair-bond and the pregnancy will make her ill."

Corday had faith things might turn out better. "She told me the pair-bond was broken. As for the pregnancy, I will take care of her."

Senator Kantor shook his head "It doesn't work that way, son."

Shooting a look at the Alpha, Corday ground his teeth. "We'll see."

"Now that you are back, the three of us need to have a discussion." Senator Kantor sat straighter, smoothing his sleeve. "Get dinner in her first; afterward the two of us will explain."

It was unsettling to be ordered around in his own home, but Corday nodded and went to the kitchen. Simple fare was prepared. There was some fresh fruit for Claire, an apple he'd bartered for a handful of batteries.

When all was ready, Corday carefully took Claire's limp hand, stroking her fingers until her bleary green eyes popped open. It was obvious she was confused. For just a moment she jerked from his nearness, ready to run. Then it began. The rich rumble of an Alpha purr took Claire from startled to angry.

The glare she gave Senator Kantor would have been funny had her scent not turned so rancid with fear. "You can stop now."

The old man conceded.

Over dinner, the men chose silence. Claire did not. "Is there another bounty?"

Corday was not going to lie to her. "Yes."

She forced down another salty bite. "And?"

"When we observed the Citadel, there was a line of citizens dragging in women of your description."

Claire cringed. "That's disgusting…"

"From what I could see, the Followers were letting them go, but citizens are starving." This was Corday's chance to explain why Senator Kantor was

232

really there. "The bounty on your head could keep a family fed for a year. We have to keep you hidden."

The old Alpha broached the greater issue. "And not just from Thólos."

Claire cocked her head. "What do you mean?"

"I need you to understand that what is said cannot leave this room."

He'd insulted her. "I never told Shepherd a thing. Never," she said.

"Dissention could be our greater enemy." Ruffling his grey hair, elbows on his knees, Kantor sighed. "Many of our people believe that unification under the Follower's governance would satisfy Shepherd. The fact is, these citizens are numerous and growing more loyal to the dictator's regime than we could have imagined. Our own ranks, even some of our brothers and sisters in arms, have been tempted to the other side. Once ensconced, they cannot be reasoned with. Your appearance within the resistance might offer too great a temptation for any straddling the line. Corday and I both believe they will vie to give you back."

"We would never let that happen, Claire," Corday interjected, desperate to explain once he saw the look on her face. "Ever. Do you understand?"

Senator Kantor dared to squeeze her hand. "We need our troops focused. We must find the contagion. To do that, you must stay hidden. No one can know you're here."

Claire sat silent, processing such information. When she finally spoke, her words were not gentle.

233

"You seem to be a wise man, Senator Kantor, but can't you see that time and further suffering will corrode those loyal to you no matter what? My pregnancy is the key to your success. So long as I am running wild in Thólos with his baby as my hostage, he won't infect the population—not at the risk of infecting me. Now is your chance to strike. Use me and rebel immediately."

"I disagree… Shepherd's treatment of you has been appalling, negligent in the gravest of ways." Solemn, Senator Kantor denied her. "If we move prematurely, he might release the contagion. I cannot risk millions of lives, your life, on a maybe. I'm sorry, Claire. Until the Red Consumption's location is uncovered, the resistance will make no move."

The line of Claire's mouth grew sharp. Sitting taller, she looked at both of them as if they were simpletons. "It's not the contagion that keeps us in his power. It's our own cowardice. Every day our people do nothing, the bastard is proving his view of our behavior is correct. The Dome is cracked. Don't you see the weather will kill us long before any virus might? *We* have to take back our city, or we die trying."

Senator Kantor put a hand on the Omega's shoulder. "Thólos' citizens are not soldiers. They're scared and have no comprehension of combat. You must understand; many are watching their families suffer, their children are dying."

Claire shook her head, swallowed her outburst. "No one in this city is a civilian anymore, there is no neutral. Either you are with Shepherd, or you are against him."

"It isn't that simple, Claire."

She looked to Senator Kantor, lost. "Isn't it?"

A deep sigh preceded Senator Kantor's explanation. "You are still young and will learn in time that things are not always as they seem."

Claire cocked her head, her previously glowing image of so highly regarded a Senator distorted by the sad impotence of such a man. "Shepherd once told me the same thing... You just echoed the words of a madman."

Senator Kantor offered a conciliatory smile, his look of pity disarming. "I'm asking you to trust me."

Corday understood what riled her; bone deep, he felt the same away. "We make progress every day, Claire. I swear it to you."

Claire looked to her friend and could see he had faith in the Alpha charged to lead the rebellion.

"I understand." And she did. She understood that the longer they waited, the more people would die—that the world was a nightmare where the men and women who'd once sworn to uphold the law might hand her back to a despot for food that would only last so long.

She understood perfectly.

She hurt; everyone hurt. And it had to end.

Once Senator Kantor had left, Corday took her hand, and led her back to the couch to rest. When he had her to himself, Corday smiled and pulled a gift out of his pocket.

"I have something to cheer you up." The Enforcer, his face dimpled, held up what was pinched between his fingers. "A few weeks ago I went to your residence. Everything was pretty smashed up, but I found this hidden under the lining of your jewelry box."

He slid a band of gold on her finger.

The gold was warm, but Claire's reaction to it utterly cold. "This was my mother's wedding ring."

As a child she'd hated the sight of it, still angry her mother had abandoned her, too young to accept what had happened. Claire had forgotten she'd even had it tucked away. Now it fit, just like her mother's disappointment in life fit. Holding up her hand to view the grim thing, she saw the correlation to her mother's impetus—a pretty, sparkling reminder that one could always choose.

"Thank you, Corday."

He took her hand again, stroked her fingers, and promised, "I want you to know that I understand the way you feel, but he's right. If the Senator's life was not gravely threatened, I don't know if I would trust even him with you."

Claire wasn't sure what to say. "Why haven't either of you asked me about Shepherd?"

Corday started to purr, scooting closer to put an arm around her shoulder. "Considering that you

236

escaped once, anything he'd allowed you to hear may have been planted to mislead the resistance should you get free again. I hate to say it, but every move that monster makes is… brilliant. There is nothing you can give us."

No one was on her side, and though she tried to hide her look of hurt, it didn't matter. Corday saw.

She chose to tell him things anyway; she needed him to hear her. "He was born in the Undercroft, his mother incarcerated by Premier Callas. His lover's name is Svana."

The Beta listened, Claire's words confirming what Brigadier Dane had conjectured. It would explain how Shepherd had been incarcerated off record, but the thought of a woman being thrown into that hell… that his own government had done such a thing, just could not be. Could it?

Claire continued, eyes far away as she blathered on. "Svana has an accent I've never heard before—like she's not from here."

"There are a thousand kilometers of snow in every direction outside this Dome, Claire. Outsiders cannot wander in."

"Just like women cannot be thrown in the Undercroft and entire cities cannot fall overnight?" To Claire it seemed there had to be more… dark truths about themselves that had to be recognized. Meeting her friend's eyes, she confessed, "I don't think Premier Callas was a good man. I'm afraid Shepherd's harsh opinion of us might not be wrong."

Corday's arm tightened around her. "Are you saying you agree with him?"

"No," she answered quickly. "No. Evil cannot change evil. Maybe his underlying motivation was once principled. I know he thinks it is, but it's not."

"That's right, Claire," Corday reaffirmed, worried to see her so lost. "Shepherd and his army are delusional."

Cheek to his shoulder, she agreed, "Aren't we all a little these days…"

Read BORN TO BE BROKEN now!

Addison Cain

USA TODAY bestselling author and Amazon Top 25 bestselling author, Addison Cain is best known for her dark romances, smoldering Omegaverse, and twisted alien worlds. Her antiheroes are not always redeemable, her lead females stand fierce, and nothing is ever as it seems.

Deep and sometimes heart wrenching, her books are not for the faint of heart. But they are just right for those who enjoy unapologetic bad boys, aggressive alphas, and a hint of violence in a kiss.

Visit her website:

addisoncain.com

Don't miss these exciting titles by Addison Cain!

The Golden Line

Wren's Song Series:

Branded Captive

Silent Captive

Broken Captive

Ravaged Captive

239

The Irdesi Empire Series:

Sigil: Book One

Sovereign: Book Two

Que: Book Three (coming soon)

The Alpha's Claim Series:

Born to be Bound

Born To Be Broken

Reborn

Stolen

Corrupted (coming soon)

A Trick of the Light Duet:

A Taste of Shine

A Shot in the Dark

Historical Romance:

Dark Side of the Sun

Horror:

Catacombs

The White Queen

Immaculate